NorthParadePublishing

©2012 North Parade Publishing Ltd.
4 North Parade,
Bath BA1 1LF .UK
Printed in China.
www.nppbooks.co.uk

This book belongs to:

....

....

....

Age ....

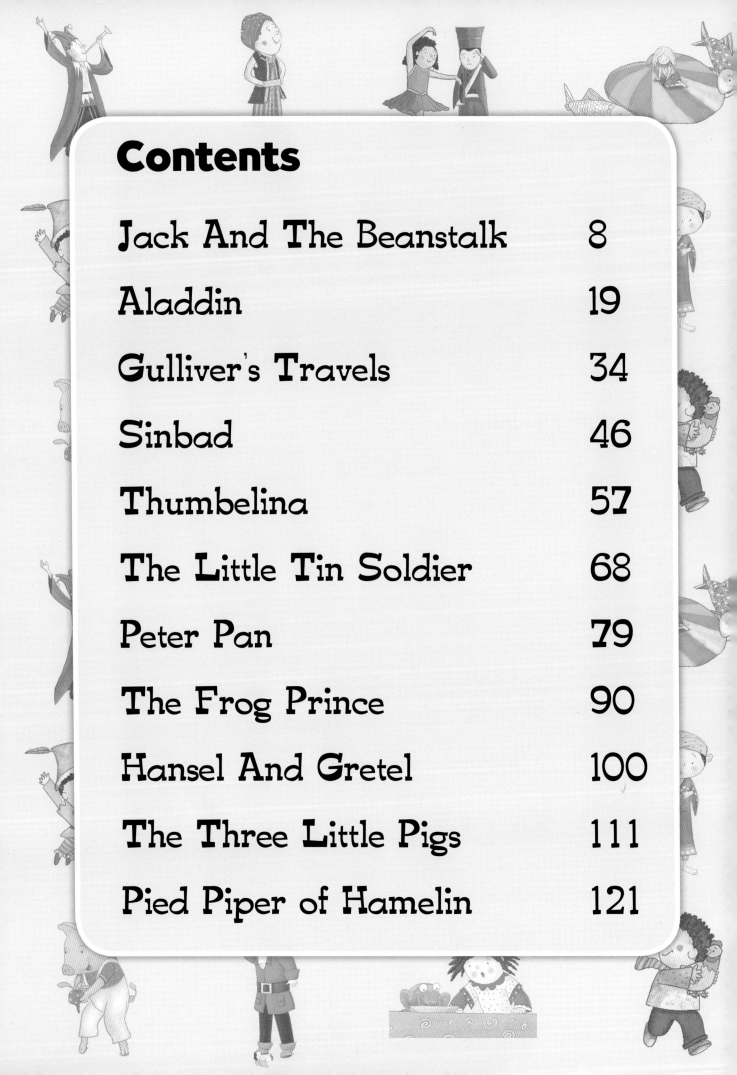

Contents

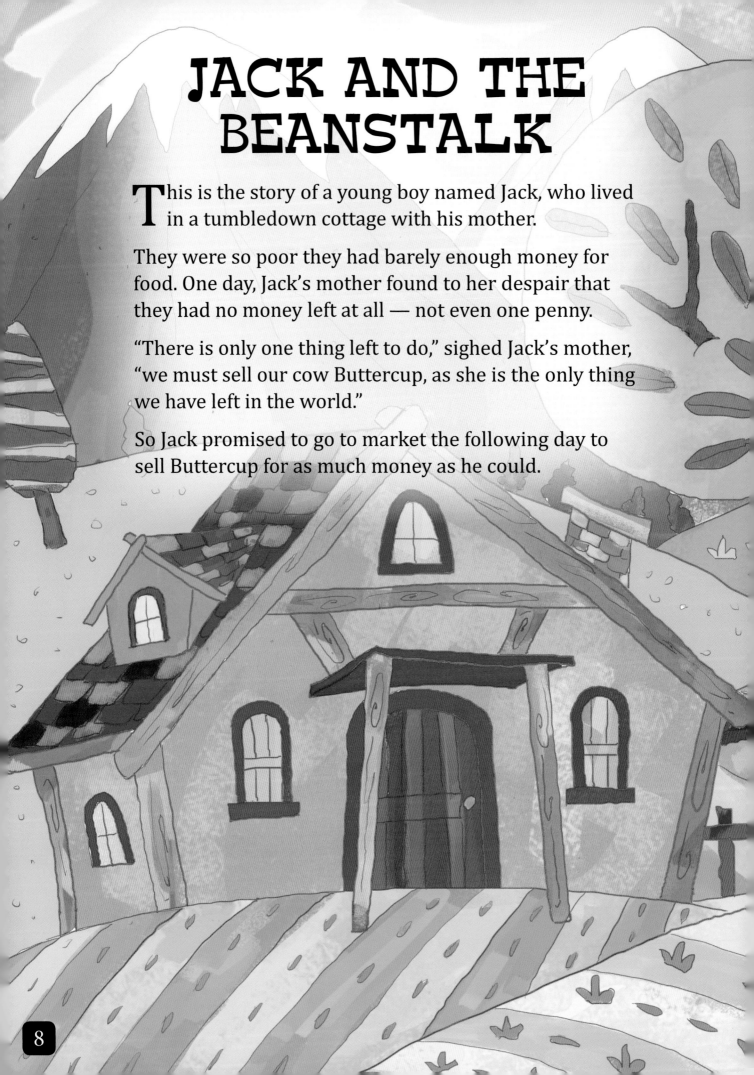

JACK AND THE BEANSTALK

This is the story of a young boy named Jack, who lived in a tumbledown cottage with his mother.

They were so poor they had barely enough money for food. One day, Jack's mother found to her despair that they had no money left at all — not even one penny.

"There is only one thing left to do," sighed Jack's mother, "we must sell our cow Buttercup, as she is the only thing we have left in the world."

So Jack promised to go to market the following day to sell Buttercup for as much money as he could.

Early next morning before it was light, Jack left for market. He crept out of the house while his mother was still asleep. She was very fond of the cow, and would have found it hard to say goodbye.

Jack hadn't gone very far along the road before he met a pedlar. "I will buy your cow in exchange for these five magic beans," the stranger said as he held out his hand. "Plant them and you will grow rich."

Young Jack couldn't resist. He gave Buttercup to the pedlar, grabbed the magic beans, and ran home to tell his mother.

She was rather surprised to see him back from the market so soon. When she heard about the magic beans, she was so angry she tossed them out of the window. And poor silly Jack was sent to bed without any supper.

The next morning dawned dark and gloomy. Jack jumped out of bed and looked out of the window. The sky above was dark — not with clouds — but with giant green leaves! To Jack's amazement the magic beans had grown in the night. They were so tall, they covered the tiny cottage and disappeared up into the sky.

Jack had to push open the cottage door with all his might. He stepped outside and began to climb the beanstalk. The branches of the bean plant were so thick they formed a ladder, and soon Jack had climbed so high that his cottage was just a tiny speck down below.

At last the branches grew thinner and Jack knew he had reached the top. Ahead of him was a long road, which led to a mysterious castle in the distance. Bravely, Jack marched along until he reached the castle door. Loudly he knocked and waited.

It was opened by the most enormous woman Jack had ever seen. "Come in and eat," her great voice boomed. "Beware my husband the Giant — or he will eat you!"

Jack turned pale. "Don't be afraid," laughed the Giantess as she led Jack into her kitchen. The kind woman gave him a plate of food almost as high as himself. Jack had only taken two mouthfuls, when the whole room began to shake.

"My husband the Giant is home," cried the Giantess, and with that, she pushed Jack into the cupboard. Not a moment too soon, for when the Giant strode into the room, he began to sniff around Jack's cupboard:

"Fee-fi-fo-fum, I smell the blood of an Englishman; Be he alive or be he dead, I'll grind his bones to make my bread." His wife smiled, "It's only the giant meat pie I cooked for your dinner that you can smell."

When he had gobbled up every scrap of food, the Giant hammered on the table with his great fists. "Wife," he called, "bring me my hen that lays golden eggs."

Jack could hardly believe his eyes when he peeped out of the cupboard.

"Lay golden eggs," commanded the Giant. And the little brown hen, which the Giant had placed on the table, began to lay golden eggs. The Giant scooped up the eggs, put them in his pocket and fell fast asleep.

Jack saw his chance. He jumped out of the cupboard, snatched up the hen and ran for his life until he reached the top of the beanstalk.

He slid down the thick branches at top speed. His mother was overjoyed to see him back safe and sound. The little brown hen laid lots of eggs and made their fortune. Jack bought back their cow, Buttercup, and all three of them were very happy.

After a while, Jack longed to climb the beanstalk once more. So early one morning, before anyone could stop him, he climbed it again in search of adventure. Higher and higher he went, until he saw the winding road he knew led to the Giant's castle.

Once again the castle door was opened by the Giant's wife. She didn't recognise Jack because of his fine new clothes, so she asked him in.

No sooner had Jack reached the kitchen, than the Giant returned. Jack looked around in panic.

"Hide in the log basket by the oven," begged the Giant's frightened wife.

Sure enough, the Giant strode straight over to where Jack was hiding. "Fee-fi-fo-fum, I smell the blood of an Englishman; Be he alive or be he dead, I'll grind his bones to make my bread."

"It's only the soup I made for you this morning," said his wife, as she placed the huge bowl on the table in front of him.

What a noise the Giant made drinking his soup! As soon as he had finished, he took down a beautiful golden harp from the shelf above him. "Play me a lullaby," the Giant commanded the golden harp. Jack had never heard such lovely music in his life. He knew he must have the harp for his very own. Such sweet music came from the harp, that the Giant soon fell into a deep sleep. Jack saw his chance and seized the harp from the table. But as he ran out of the castle gates, the harp began to play loudly, "Help me, Master. Help me!"

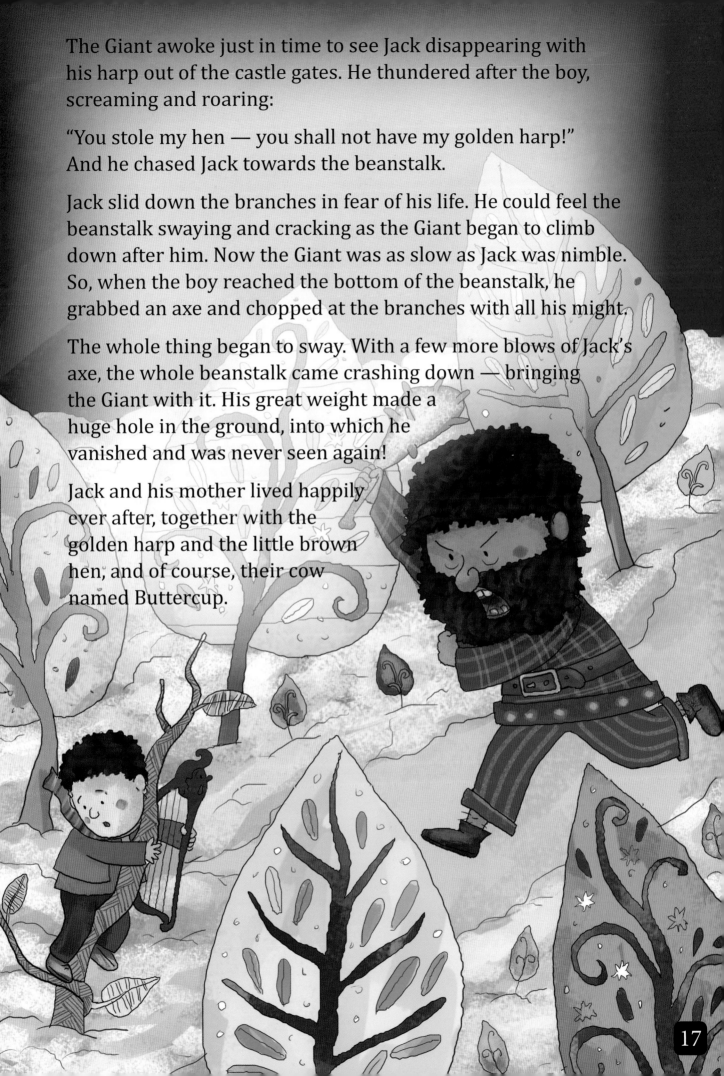

The Giant awoke just in time to see Jack disappearing with his harp out of the castle gates. He thundered after the boy, screaming and roaring:

"You stole my hen — you shall not have my golden harp!" And he chased Jack towards the beanstalk.

Jack slid down the branches in fear of his life. He could feel the beanstalk swaying and cracking as the Giant began to climb down after him. Now the Giant was as slow as Jack was nimble. So, when the boy reached the bottom of the beanstalk, he grabbed an axe and chopped at the branches with all his might.

The whole thing began to sway. With a few more blows of Jack's axe, the whole beanstalk came crashing down — bringing the Giant with it. His great weight made a huge hole in the ground, into which he vanished and was never seen again!

Jack and his mother lived happily ever after, together with the golden harp and the little brown hen, and of course, their cow named Buttercup.

Aladdin

This strange story happened in a far-off country many years ago. It is a tale of a magic lamp, a magic ring, an evil magician and many more amazing things. But most of all, it is a story about a boy called Aladdin.

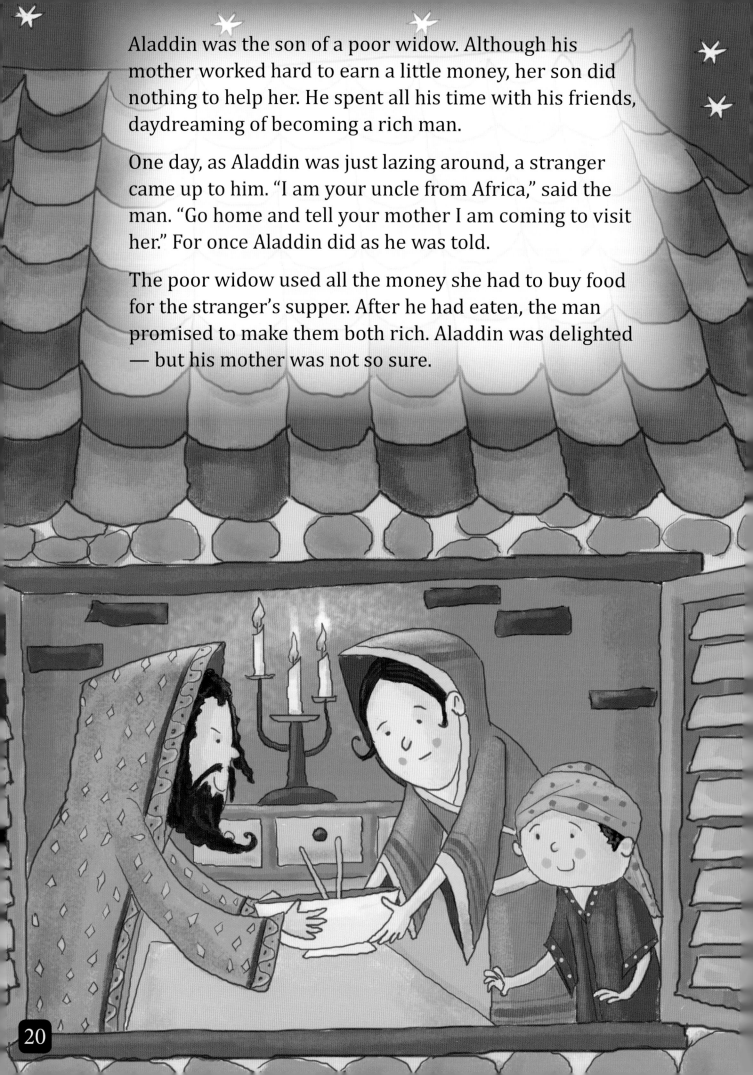

Aladdin was the son of a poor widow. Although his mother worked hard to earn a little money, her son did nothing to help her. He spent all his time with his friends, daydreaming of becoming a rich man.

One day, as Aladdin was just lazing around, a stranger came up to him. "I am your uncle from Africa," said the man. "Go home and tell your mother I am coming to visit her." For once Aladdin did as he was told.

The poor widow used all the money she had to buy food for the stranger's supper. After he had eaten, the man promised to make them both rich. Aladdin was delighted — but his mother was not so sure.

"All I ask," said the stranger, "is that Aladdin do one small task for me tomorrow in return."

Now as you may have guessed, the stranger was not Aladdin's uncle at all. He was really a powerful magician in disguise. He was not out to help Aladdin — but trick him.

Very early next morning, Aladdin and the magician left the city. By the time it was light they had reached the mountains. As they climbed up and up, the path grew narrower with steep rocks on each side.

At long last they stopped. They could go no farther for a huge boulder blocked their path.

Aladdin sat down to rest, but not for long! The magician pointed a long finger at the boulder and shouted, "Abracadabra". A noise like thunder echoed round the mountains, the boulder vanished, and the rock behind cracked in two.

The magician grabbed hold of Aladdin. "Go through that crack in the rock, because I am too big. You will find some steps which lead to a cave, in the cave you will see an old lamp. Bring it to me straight away."

Poor Aladdin tried to run away, but the evil magician held him too tightly. "If you are such a coward," bellowed the magician, "take my magic ring." And with that he pushed Aladdin through the crack in the rock, and the poor boy fell down the steps and into the cave.

When Aladdin picked himself up, he could hardly believe his eyes. The cave was full of gold and jewels. Aladdin gasped. He picked up a few and stuffed them in his pocket to take back to his mother.

Outside the cave the magician began to shout, "Bring me my lamp at once!" But Aladdin was too busy to hear him.

Because Aladdin did not obey him at once, the magician flew into a terrible rage. He shouted the magic word "Abracadabra" and the crack in the rock closed and Aladdin was trapped.

The poor boy buried his head in his hands in despair. Now quite by chance he rubbed the magic ring on his finger. Immediately the cave was filled with a loud swishing noise, and an enormous genie appeared. "I'm the Genie of the Ring, O Master! Speak, and I obey!" "Take me home," gasped Aladdin.

"Your wish is my command," answered the genie. "But first, O Master, take this old lamp. Inside is a genie more powerful than me, and you will become his master."

A great roaring sound filled the air, and Aladdin found himself being carried back home by a genie twice as large as the first one.

Aladdin's mother screamed with fright, until he told her of his adventures and the wonderful lamp.

At last Aladdin's dream had come true and they were no longer poor. He soon became the richest man in the land, thanks to the Genie of the Lamp. The Emperor became his friend and invited him to his court.

One day Aladdin met the Emperor's daughter, and he fell in love with her at once. Aladdin dare not ask the Emperor if he could marry the Princess. So he rubbed the lamp and asked the genie to fill the whole of the Emperor's garden with treasure.

Then the Emperor gladly gave his consent. Aladdin rubbed his lamp again, and a beautiful new palace appeared for Aladdin and the Princess to live in.

Far away in Africa, the evil magician heard about Aladdin's palace. He guessed at once that Aladdin had the lamp.

Straight away he travelled to China. He disguised himself as an old lamp-seller and waited by the gates of Aladdin's palace. "New lamps for old," he cried loudly. He didn't have to wait long before a servant brought out all the old lamps from the palace.

The evil magician saw his lamp and grabbed it with glee. He ordered the genie to take him, the palace and the Princess back to his home in Africa.

When Aladdin returned home he could find no trace of his Princess or his palace.

As he sat wondering what to do, quite by accident he rubbed the magic ring. At once the genie appeared. "Take me to my Princess, O Genie of the Ring!" Aladdin begged.

Before he could even blink, he found himself
standing outside her bedroom window.
The Princess was overjoyed to see Aladdin.
"I know where the lamp is," she whispered.
"The magician keeps it tied to his belt night
and day."

Quickly Aladdin told her his plan. "Take this
sleeping powder and mix it in his wine. You
must steal the lamp as soon as he falls asleep!"

Late that night the Princess dropped the powder into the Magician's glass, although she was very frightened. He fell asleep at once and she carefully untied the lamp.

Aladdin jumped out from his hiding place and grabbed the lamp. One rub and the genie appeared. "Take us all home!" Aladdin cried.

The genie's magic was so powerful, he was able to whisk the palace, the Princess, Aladdin and all the servants back home to China.

"Drop that evil magician into the sea on the way home!" ordered Aladdin.

The Emperor and Aladdin's mother were waiting to welcome them all back home. At last their adventures were over. As for the lamp, Aladdin made sure it was kept in a very safe place — and never given away again.

GULLIVER'S TRAVELS

This is the story of Lemuel Gulliver, a man who lived about two hundred and fifty years ago. He studied very hard and after many years, he became a doctor. He longed to travel and loved the sea, so he became a doctor on board a sailing ship.

One day he set off on a long voyage to the South Seas on a ship called the Antelope — and here begins one of the strangest adventure stories ever told.

All went well on the Antelope for the first few weeks.
Then suddenly one night, a great storm sprang up,
the ship hit a rock and was wrecked.

Although the sea was rough and the waves high, Gulliver
was such a strong swimmer that he managed to reach the
shore. Completely exhausted, he dragged himself up the
beach as far away from the sea as possible. He lay down
on the first grassy bank he found and fell into a deep sleep.

At daybreak, when he opened his eyes, he tried to sit up
and look around — but he was tied to the ground! He
couldn't move his arms or legs or even lift his head.

Then Gulliver felt something alive running up his legs and across his chest — like a crowd of mice or several beetles perhaps!

All at once, Gulliver let out a great roar of surprise. For standing on his chest were at least forty men, each about six inches high. Gulliver's great roar startled the little men. Quickly they slid down to the floor below, where great crowds of tiny people were assembled.

As Gulliver tried to turn his head to look, the strings that bound his arms snapped. This frightened the little people so much, that they shot hundreds of their sharp arrows into his face.

Although this hurt quite a bit, Gulliver decided to lie still and not to frighten the little people again. After a while, when they had walked all over Gulliver, they became quite brave and tried to talk to him. But the little folk spoke a different language, so Gulliver couldn't understand a single word.

Somehow their tiny Emperor realised that the giant man they had captured must be very hungry by now. So he gave orders that a tall wooden platform be built, to reach Gulliver's mouth.

After a while several cart loads of food and wine arrived. And hundreds of the tiny men climbed up the platform with baskets of bread and meat. The hungry Gulliver drank a whole barrel of their wine in one gulp, and ate a basket full of loaves in one bite.

The Lilliputians (for that is what the little people were called) kept bringing more and more until Gulliver was so full up he fell fast asleep.

The little people seemed to have lost all fear of the gigantic Gulliver, so while he slept, thousands of them set to work. Five hundred carpenters made a platform on wheels, and nine hundred men hoisted the sleeping Gulliver onto it. Then with five hundred guards either side and one thousand five hundred horses pulling hard, they began to move him towards their capital city.

It took a whole day and night to reach their destination. At last the procession came to a halt outside a large church, which was to be Gulliver's house — although it seemed as small as a dog kennel to him.

The tiny Emperor of Lilliput did not intend to set Gulliver free altogether. He ordered all his blacksmiths to make a thick chain and padlock it onto Gulliver's leg, so he could move around— but not very far.

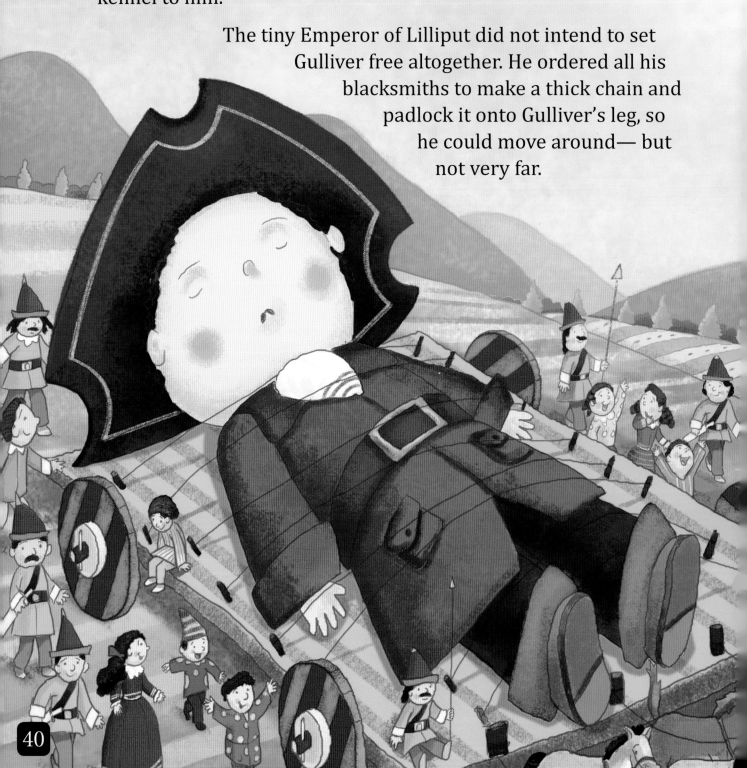

News soon spread of the giant the Emperor had captured. People flocked in from all over the land of Lilliput, until the city was jammed with the little folk.

Six hundred of them were chosen to look after Gulliver, and four hundred tailors were kept busy making him new clothes. Six of Lilliput's finest scholars were sent to teach him their language.

At last the Emperor could understand Gulliver when he asked to be set free. He finally agreed, on one condition. Gulliver must empty his pockets of anything that could be dangerous to Lilliput.

Out came a knife, a comb and a razor. The little people were fascinated. Then came his handkerchief — which to them looked like a carpet. His snuffbox seemed like a huge chest of gunpowder; his watch made more noise than a water mill, and they thought that his purse was a fishing net.

Finally Gulliver took out his pistol and fired it into the air. So great was the noise, thousands of the little people fell flat on their backs with shock. Only the Emperor stood his ground. For a man only six inches high, he was very brave.

But even the brave Emperor feared something. And one day he came to ask Gulliver's help. On the nearby island of Blefuscu lived people called the Big-Endians. Their fleet of fifty ships had just set sail to invade Lilliput.

What a shock the poor Big-Endian sailors got when Gulliver waded out to sea, roped all their ships together, and dragged them back to Lilliput.

It didn't take Gulliver very long to realise that the Emperor of Lilliput was only using him to fight his battle for him, and that the Big-Endians were not a wicked people at all. So Gulliver made up his mind to go over to their island and live with them.

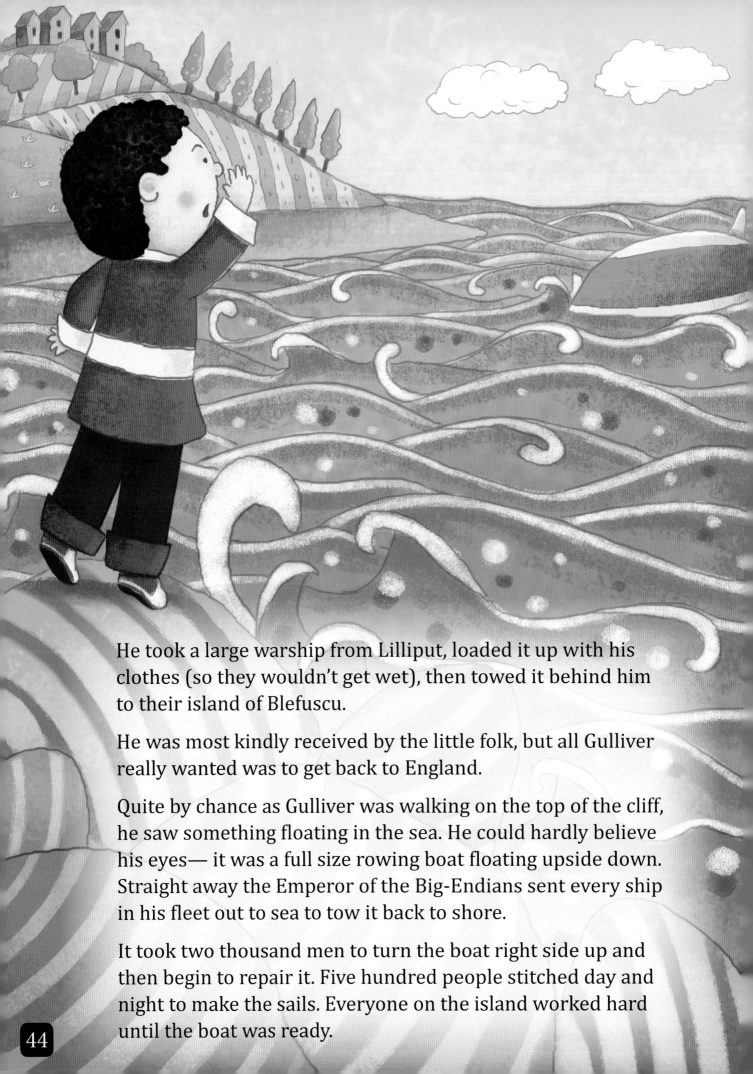

He took a large warship from Lilliput, loaded it up with his clothes (so they wouldn't get wet), then towed it behind him to their island of Blefuscu.

He was most kindly received by the little folk, but all Gulliver really wanted was to get back to England.

Quite by chance as Gulliver was walking on the top of the cliff, he saw something floating in the sea. He could hardly believe his eyes— it was a full size rowing boat floating upside down. Straight away the Emperor of the Big-Endians sent every ship in his fleet out to sea to tow it back to shore.

It took two thousand men to turn the boat right side up and then begin to repair it. Five hundred people stitched day and night to make the sails. Everyone on the island worked hard until the boat was ready.

Gulliver took on board several tiny live sheep and cows to take back home. Then sadly came the time to say farewell.

After only two days at sea, Gulliver was picked up by a sailing ship heading for England. When he told his strange story, the captain could hardly believe it— until he saw the tiny cows and sheep which Gulliver placed on the table in front of him.

At last Gulliver returned home. People were delighted to welcome him back, and never tired of hearing his strange story.

SINBAD

Once upon a time, in the faraway city of Bagdad, there lived a young man whose name was Sinbad. He longed for adventure, and that is why he sailed the seven seas.

One day, Sinbad sailed away on one of many journeys. After many days at sea, his ship dropped anchor at a tiny island, and Sinbad and the other sailors stepped ashore to look around.

All at once, the island seemed to grow and rise up out of the water. It was no island, but a monster whale! Suddenly, the whale took a great dive beneath the waves, and everyone fell off into the sea.

All the other sailors managed to swim back to the ship, but poor Sinbad was left behind floating in the water, clinging to a piece of driftwood.

After a while he was washed ashore on another island. He ran across the sandy beach and climbed the tallest palm tree, to try to see his ship. But alas, Sinbad had been left all alone, and his ship was nowhere to be seen.

As he gazed down from the tree, Sinbad noticed a huge white egg on the sand. He slid down the trunk to take a better look. All of a sudden, a big black shadow passed over him. There, circling overhead, was a great white bird — almost as big as the island.

"Now's my chance to escape," thought Sinbad. And when the great white bird flew down onto its egg, Sinbad unwound his turban and tied himself onto the bird's gigantic leg.

Sure enough, the bird flew off carrying Sinbad with him. His plan had worked. The great bird flew high into the air, through deep valleys, and over mountains, until at last it landed, and Sinbad could untie his turban and escape.

The boy found himself in a dry river bed, surrounded by steep cliffs too difficult to climb. He was trapped again.

"How did I get myself into this mess?" Sinbad cried out loudly, his voice echoing around the cliffs.

All of a sudden, there came a loud hissing noise. All around poor Sinbad large serpents slithered across the floor. Underneath the snakes were huge diamonds and gems— some as big as Sinbad himself. At the sight of so much treasure, Sinbad's eyes opened wide. Then he remembered the snakes and ran to the nearest cave for safety.

"I can hear voices," cried Sinbad in delight. "Someone is here to rescue me." The boy looked up and saw faces peering over the edge of the cliffs. Men were throwing something onto the rocks below. Could it be huge pieces of meat?

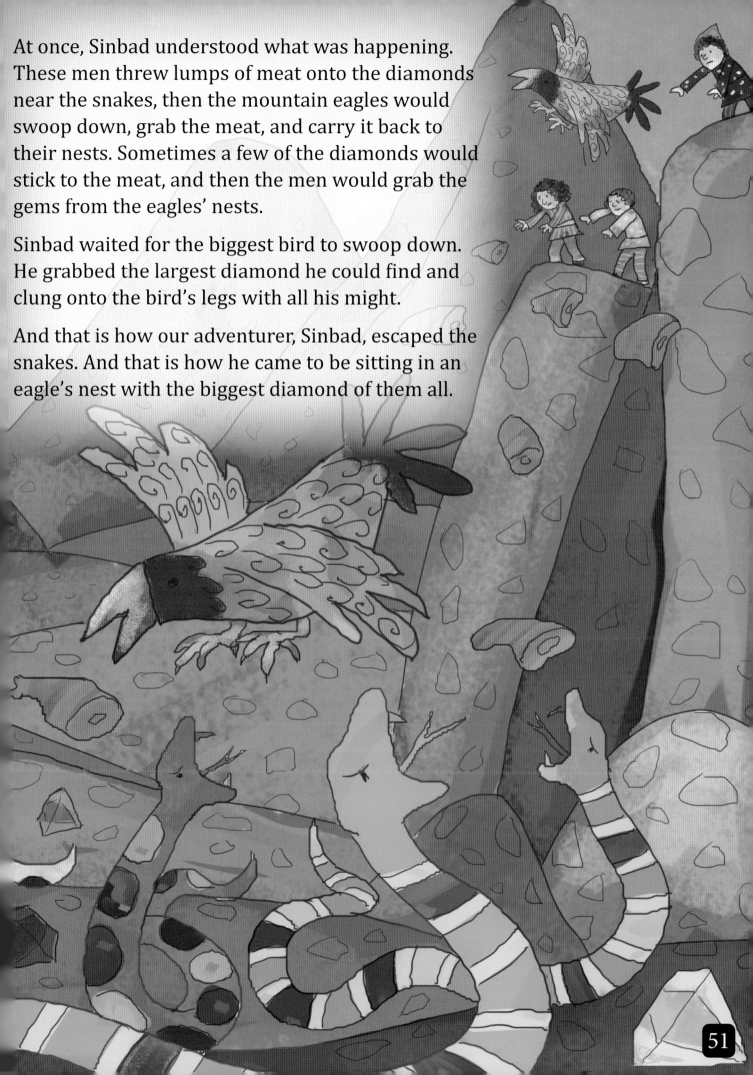

At once, Sinbad understood what was happening. These men threw lumps of meat onto the diamonds near the snakes, then the mountain eagles would swoop down, grab the meat, and carry it back to their nests. Sometimes a few of the diamonds would stick to the meat, and then the men would grab the gems from the eagles' nests.

Sinbad waited for the biggest bird to swoop down. He grabbed the largest diamond he could find and clung onto the bird's legs with all his might.

And that is how our adventurer, Sinbad, escaped the snakes. And that is how he came to be sitting in an eagle's nest with the biggest diamond of them all.

51

Sinbad returned home a rich man. After a while he got tired of doing nothing and made up his mind to set sail on another voyage. After many days at sea, his ship dropped anchor in the harbour of a large city.

When the people saw Sinbad and his crew, they begged him for help. "Our markets are quite empty of fruit. We have nothing to sell and nothing to buy," they moaned. "We have no coconuts or dates, no pomegranates or figs, not even one banana."

Sinbad looked puzzled, until the people explained, "Our trees are so tall and smooth, it is impossible for anyone to climb them, except the monkeys."

"Leave it to us," laughed Sinbad and his sailors. And they set off to find the trees in the forest.

When the ship's crew saw the monkeys who lived in the top branches, it gave them an idea. The sailors looked around for stones, which they threw at the monkeys, who thought it was some sort of game.

The mischievous monkeys pelted the sailors with coconuts and fruit, who, in turn, filled up great sacks with them .

They returned to the city and gave the food to the hungry people. Everyone was very grateful and Sinbad and his crew sailed away with many presents and thanks from the city.

No sooner had Sinbad gone back home to Bagdad, than the Caliph sent for him. "Set sail at once," he commanded, "and take these gifts to my friend the Sultan of Tasmir Island."

So once more, Sinbad and his crew put to sea, but alas, on the way, the ship was attacked by pirates, who captured all on board. At the very next port these cruel pirates sold Sinbad and his crew as slaves.

Sinbad was bought by a wealthy merchant who had a lovely daughter. "Slave," grinned the merchant, "I have a very dangerous task for you," and he dragged Sinbad deep into the forest.

"In a few moments the biggest elephant in the world will pass this way to drink at the river. Take this bow and arrow and shoot him," and at that, the merchant pushed Sinbad up a tree and ran away.

All at once, Sinbad could feel the trees shaking. Thundering down the path came an enormous elephant with gleaming tusks. Sinbad shook with fright!

The poor boy trembled so much that he lost his balance and fell out of the tree. He landed on top of the elephant and slid down his trunk onto the ground. Sinbad closed his eyes tight, for he was certain the elephant's great foot would crush him to a pulp. A soft voice was speaking to the great elephant, it was the merchant's daughter. She was standing in the middle of the forest patch — feeding him bread and fruit from a silver dish. Sinbad could hardly believe his eyes. "Don't be afraid," said the girl. "I come here every night to feed this beautiful creature. My father is a cruel man.

"He wants to kill my elephant and cut off his tusks to sell for ivory." When the girl put her arms around the beast's great trunk, Sinbad could see how gentle the elephant was.

"Come," smiled Sinbad, "let us escape from here." Quickly he helped the girl onto the elephant. "We will ride away this very night on the elephant's back, and he will carry us back home to Bagdad." So off they went together travelling over many miles and many lands, until they arrived back safely ... and lived happily ever after.

THUMBELINA

There was once a woman who lived all alone. Her cottage stood by itself in the heart of the countryside, far from neighbours and friends.

She was very lonely and longed for someone to keep her company. "I wish I had a little child of my own," the woman said out loud, as she worked in her garden.

It just so happened that an old witch was passing by and heard her. She fumbled in the folds of her cloak and took out one small seed, "This is a magic seed. Plant it and see what grows." And with that the witch vanished.

As the woman was very fond of flowers, she planted the seed carefully in a pot and placed it on her kitchen window.

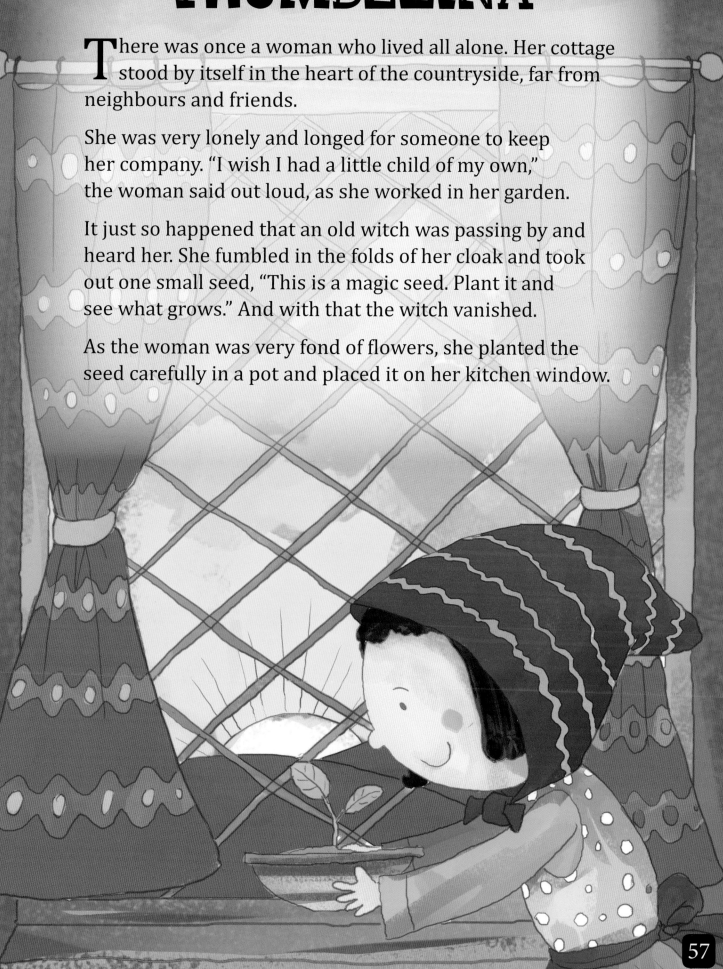

In no time at all, a green shoot appeared. By the next day a tall stalk had grown with a flower bud at the top.

When the woman bent down to admire it, the flower bud burst open. Sitting right in the middle of the petals was a tiny girl— no bigger than a thumb. The woman smiled, "I think I shall call you, Thumbelina."

So tiny was the little girl, that half a walnut shell was just the right size for her bed. Her covers were made of rose petals with a soft rose bud for a pillow. A daisy made a perfect hat, and a violet leaf made a fine umbrella.

The woman took great care to see that her beloved Thumbelina came to no harm.

One warm night as she lay fast asleep in her walnut bed, an ugly toad peered through the window. "She'll make a perfect, wife for my son," he croaked.

And he grabbed Thumbelina in her walnut shell bed and jumped out of the window.

The ugly toad hopped and hopped far away through the darkness, taking great care not to wake little Thumbelina.

When he reached his home in the mud of the river bank, he showed Thumbelina to his son — who was twice as ugly as his father!

The two toads swam with the walnut shell bed into the middle of the river, and placed it on a lily pad. "Tomorrow you can get married," croaked the old toad to his son.

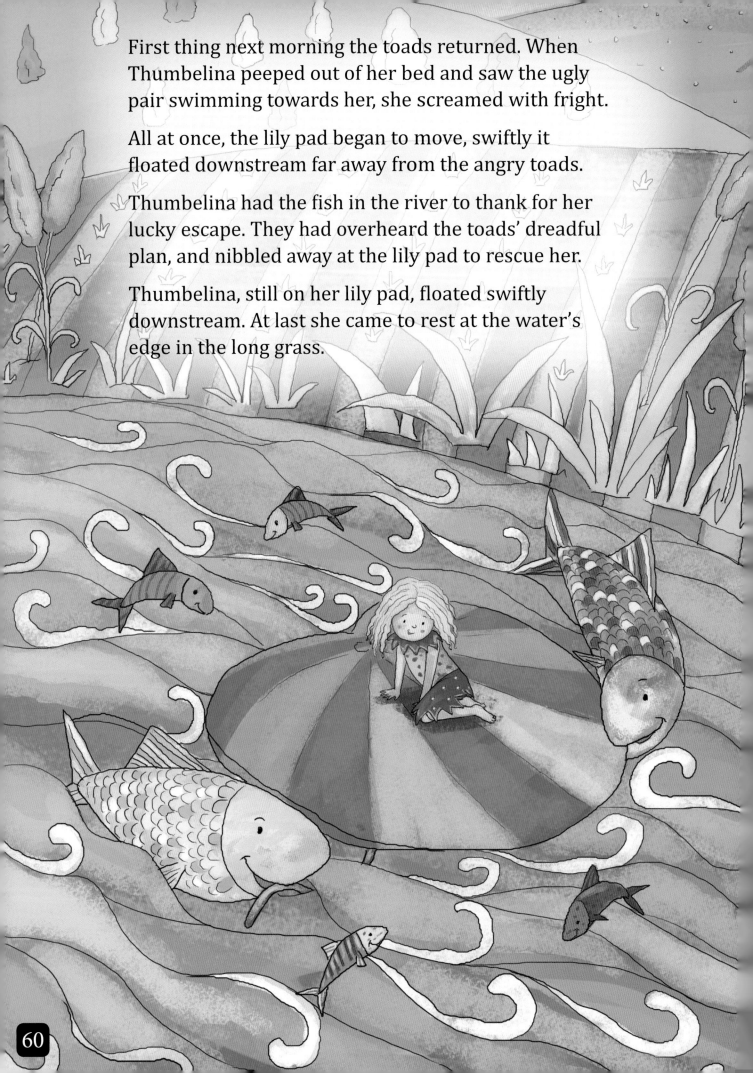

First thing next morning the toads returned. When Thumbelina peeped out of her bed and saw the ugly pair swimming towards her, she screamed with fright.

All at once, the lily pad began to move, swiftly it floated downstream far away from the angry toads.

Thumbelina had the fish in the river to thank for her lucky escape. They had overheard the toads' dreadful plan, and nibbled away at the lily pad to rescue her.

Thumbelina, still on her lily pad, floated swiftly downstream. At last she came to rest at the water's edge in the long grass.

Just at that moment, a big black beetle flew overhead. He swooped down and carried the tiny girl off into the wood to be his bride.

How the other beetles laughed when they saw Thumbelina. "Where are her wings?" the lady beetles cried. "And why has she only got two legs instead of six?" they scoffed.

All this jeering made the big black beetle feel ashamed of Thumbelina. So he flew away, leaving her alone in the wood.

Happily, the little girl soon found new friends all around her. Squirrels and rabbits came to her with their torn jackets and holey socks to mend. The birds and mice often asked her to baby-sit with their young ones.

In return they brought her food. The bees buzzed by with honey and she found juicy berries and nuts everywhere.

61

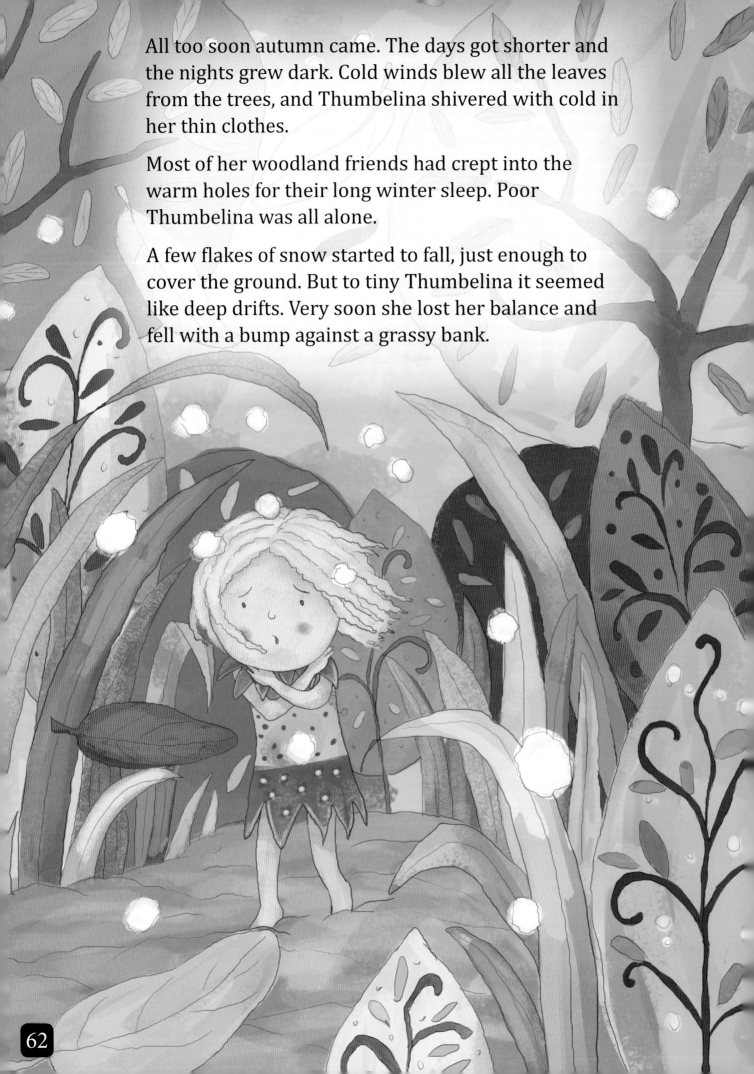

All too soon autumn came. The days got shorter and the nights grew dark. Cold winds blew all the leaves from the trees, and Thumbelina shivered with cold in her thin clothes.

Most of her woodland friends had crept into the warm holes for their long winter sleep. Poor Thumbelina was all alone.

A few flakes of snow started to fall, just enough to cover the ground. But to tiny Thumbelina it seemed like deep drifts. Very soon she lost her balance and fell with a bump against a grassy bank.

"Who's that knocking on my door?" squeaked a friendly fieldmouse, as he held his lantern high. There in its bright beam he saw Thumbelina, shivering with cold and very hungry. "Come inside into my warm parlour and have some food, you poor creature," the fieldmouse said kindly.

Thumbelina liked the fieldmouse so much, and found his house so comfortable, that she agreed to stay all winter.

How quickly the winter months passed by. Thumbelina cooked and cleaned for the mouse, and in the long evenings she told him lovely stories.

One afternoon the fieldmouse invited his neighbour, the mole, to tea. The tiny girl baked a chocolate cake, and took great care to serve the visitor properly.

The mole was a handsome fellow, with a black velvet coat and very good manners. To her great surprise, after he had eaten the last piece of cake, the mole asked Thumbelina to marry him. "I don't want to marry anyone," cried Thumbelina with dismay.

All the same the mole invited Thumbelina to see his house underground. They followed the mole through many dark tunnels and passages. The mole loved to live underground, and never went out in the sunshine. Thumbelina trembled. She would hate to live in the dark and never see the light again.

All of a sudden she stumbled over something soft lying on the floor of the tunnel. "It's only a swallow who has died from the cold," the mole shouted over his shoulder. But Thumbelina was sure she could feel the bird's heart beating.

Later that night, when the fieldmouse was asleep, she fetched a blanket and some warm milk, which soon made the swallow feel better.

She cared for him all winter long. And when spring came, he was ready to fly away.

The swallow pleaded with Thumbelina to fly away with him. "If only I could," she sighed. "But the fieldmouse has begged me to marry the mole tomorrow. He has been so good and kind to me that I must agree." So sadly the two friends parted.

Feeling very unhappy, Thumbelina asked the if she might go out in the sunshine for the last time before she married the mole.

As she stepped outside, the swallow swept down from the sky. This was her last chance of freedom. Thumbelina jumped on the bird's back and the swallow carried her home to her cottage.

At long last everyone was together again and happy once more.

THE LITTLE TIN SOLDIER

Once upon a time, there lived an old toymaker. Folk came from miles around to gaze in his shop window full of toys, and sometimes they would call in and buy presents for their children.

One day, the old toymaker melted down a very large tin spoon. Carefully he poured the hot metal into some special moulds to make a set of tin soldiers. He filled up twenty of the moulds, but on the twenty — first he ran out of tin.

So when the soldiers were turned out, twenty were exactly alike— but the very last soldier had one leg missing.

With great skill, the old toymaker painted the soldiers. He gave them red tunics and blue trousers and finished off their hats with gold braid. They looked splendid standing stiffly to attention and saluting. Even the tin soldier with one leg stood up just as straight as the others, looking every bit as brave and dashing. The old man was pleased with his work. And it wasn't too long before someone saw the twenty-one tin soldiers in his window, and bought them.

The box full of soldiers were given to a small boy for his birthday, and when he lifted the lid, he was thrilled to bits. "Tin soldiers," he gasped. "Just what I've always wanted."

The boy stood all his soldiers in a row in his nursery without even noticing that one of them had only one leg.

The little tin soldier gazed around him at the other toys. The floor below was littered with teddy bears, clockwork toys, bricks and dolls and a toy fort for the tin soldiers.

But the best toy was a splendid cardboard castle. It had tall pillars either side of the door, and more windows than the tin soldier could count. On the steps of the cardboard castle stood a graceful ballerina doll. She was balanced perfectly on one leg with the other stretched behind her — it looked as if she had only one leg.

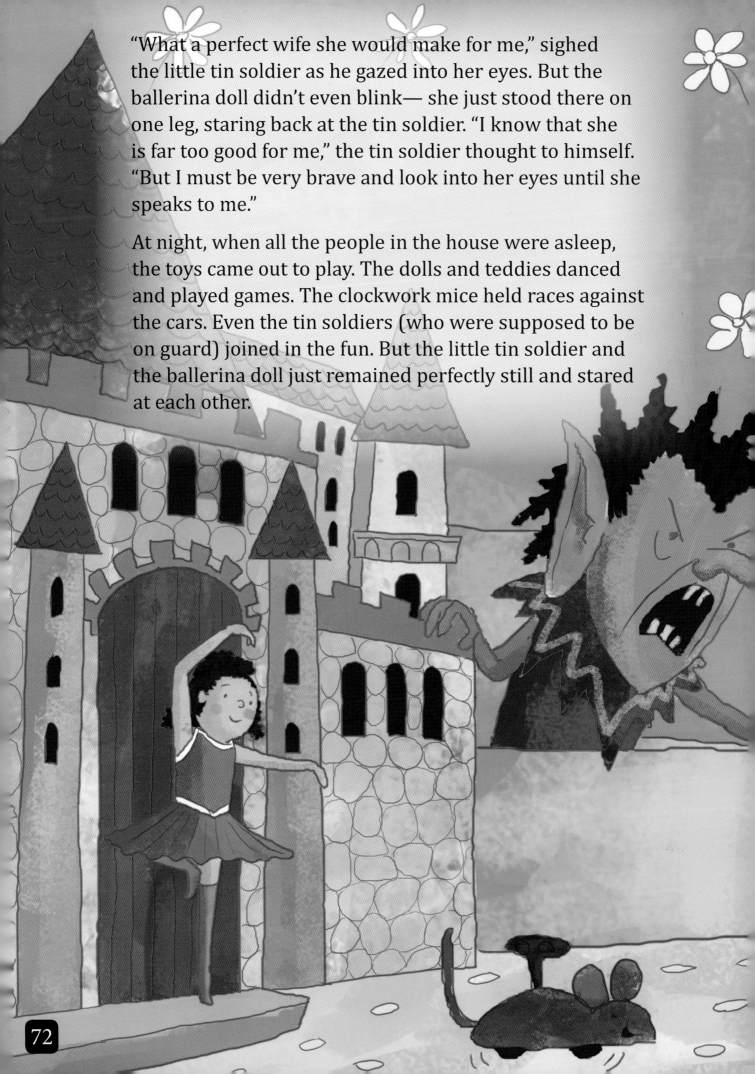

"What a perfect wife she would make for me," sighed the little tin soldier as he gazed into her eyes. But the ballerina doll didn't even blink— she just stood there on one leg, staring back at the tin soldier. "I know that she is far too good for me," the tin soldier thought to himself. "But I must be very brave and look into her eyes until she speaks to me."

At night, when all the people in the house were asleep, the toys came out to play. The dolls and teddies danced and played games. The clockwork mice held races against the cars. Even the tin soldiers (who were supposed to be on guard) joined in the fun. But the little tin soldier and the ballerina doll just remained perfectly still and stared at each other.

Suddenly one night, the clock in the nursery struck midnight. The jack-in-the-box flew open and a bad-tempered goblin flew out. He pointed a honey finger at the tin soldier. "Stop staring at the ballerina or it will be the worse for you," he snarled.

Although the goblin gave the tin soldier a terrible fright, he bravely stood to attention and continued to gaze at the ballerina doll.

Very early next morning the little boy came into his nursery to play with his soldiers. He lined them up in a row on the window ledge, then ran off to have his breakfast.

Without any warning, the little tin soldier was whisked
through the air. He fell out of the open window, and down
into the street below... Who knows how it happened? It may
have been just a gust of wind or even that nasty goblin.
No-one will ever know!

As the poor tin soldier lay upside down in the gutter it
began to pour with rain. Two little boys came running
past, and one of them spotted the tin soldier. The other had
made a paper boat, so they stood the soldier in the front
and carefully launched it into the gutter.

Swiftly the boat sped along the water until it was swept into a drain beneath the street. The brave tin soldier showed no fear, even when the boat sailed out of the drain and into the river. Then it began to sink!

All too soon the water was up to the soldier's chest. The paper boat became so soggy that it just fell to pieces, and the tin soldier sank beneath the surface.

What a brave tin soldier he was! He showed no fear at all, even when the biggest fish in the river swallowed him up. It was terribly dark and gloomy inside the fish's stomach. The brave tin soldier kept his spirits up by thinking about the lovely ballerina, and how he must see her once more.

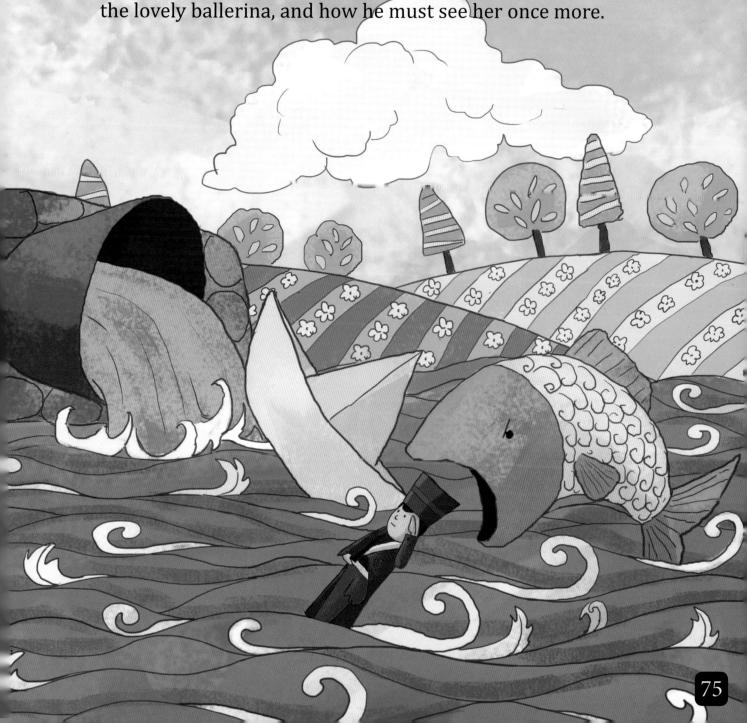

One day, the great fish was caught with a rod and line, and ended up on a kitchen table. As the cook cut open the fish with her sharp knife, the brave tin soldier fell out onto the table. The startled cook picked him up and took him up to the nursery.

Now it was the tin soldier's turn to be surprised. He found himself in the very same nursery with the very same toys: the dolls, the teddies, all his soldier friends — and best of all, his lovely and best of all, his lovely ballerina doll, but neither of them said one word.

That night, when all was quiet, the brave tin soldier slowly made his way to the cardboard castle. He was going to beg the ballerina to come away with him.

As he reached her side the jack-in-the-box lid flew open, and the goblin pushed the brave tin soldier backwards. How dreadful! The poor tin soldier fell straight into the fire.

Then something very strange happened. The nursery door opened and the sudden draught blew the ballerina doll into the arms of the tin soldier. The fire flared up and both melted away together in the flames.

Next morning, when the fire had cooled, the maid came to clear out the ashes. All she found was a little piece of tin in the shape of a heart.

PETER PAN

Here is the story of Peter Pan — the boy who never wants to grow up. He comes from Never-Never Land, an island which children sometimes visit in their dreams. The most magical thing about Peter Pan is ... he can fly!

This favourite of all stories begins in a large house in London. It's the home of Mr. and Mrs. Darling, parents of Wendy, Michael and John. Now, these three children have a very unusual nurse, a great big Newfoundland dog called Nana!

Why, you might ask, did Peter Pan ever visit the home of the Darlings? Sometimes, when he was feeling lonely, he would fly up to their nursery window and peep inside — just to be part of a human family again and remember what it was like to have a mother.

If the nursery window was left open and Nana the dog was nowhere about, Peter would fly right into the nursery. Wendy often caught a glimpse of the strange boy — but she thought she was just dreaming.

Now one night, Mrs. Darling was sitting sewing while her children slept. Peter flew straight in through the window. He didn't notice that Nana was in the nursery. The dog sprang up and growled and snarled at the boy. As he tried to escape, his shadow caught on the window and Peter had to leave it behind. Rather startled, Mrs. Darling picked it up and put it in a drawer.

The very next night when the Darlings were asleep, a tiny bright light flew in through the window and began to dart about — it was Tinker Bell, a tiny fairy who went everywhere with Peter Pan.

She was searching for Peter's shadow. She looked in all the cupboards, all the drawers, she even delved inside a jug. Eventually she found the right place just as Peter flew in through the window.

He grabbed his shadow and shut the drawer tight, trapping poor Tinker Bell inside. He searched around trying to find something that would stick his shadow back on. All this noise woke up Wendy. She knew what to do straight away. She fetched her workbox, and very neatly stitched the shadow on again.

When Wendy offered Peter a kiss he looked puzzled. He had never had a kiss before and held his hand out for a present. So Wendy gave him her silver thimble instead. In return, Peter gave her one of his acorn-shaped buttons, which Wendy hung on a chain round her neck. As Peter sat in the nursery he told Wendy all about Never-Never Land where he lived with the Lost Boys and the fairies. He explained to her how a fairy dies every time a human child says, "I do not believe in fairies!"

It was then that Peter remembered Tinker Bell still trapped in the drawer. He let her out, and she was furious. She buzzed round Wendy and tried to pull her hair. Perhaps she was jealous of Peter's new friend!

All this noise woke up John and Michael. They listened spellbound when Peter told them about his fierce fights with the pirates on Never-Never Land. And, of course, they wanted to go.

So it was agreed that they should first learn to fly, and go away with Peter Pan that very night.

After a great deal of practise they were ready. Not a moment too soon, for running up the stairs came Mr. and Mrs. Darling.

One by one the children flew out of the nursery window, leaving their poor parents behind. Soon they were soaring through the night sky with the lights of London far below them.

On and on they went. "Second star to the right and on until morning," cried Peter Pan as he sped ahead.

At long last, as the sun rose, they glimpsed Never-Never Land beneath them. It was just as Peter had said.

Anchored near the island was the pirate ship, the Jolly Roger, with its evil Captain Hook. The pirate chief hated Pan because he had cut off his hand and thrown it to a crocodile, who longed to eat the rest of him. Luckily the crocodile had swallowed a clock, and everyone could hear him coming with his loud 'tick, tick, tick'.

As they flew over the island, Wendy and the boys saw an Indian tribe round their wigwams. These were the Indians who were always on the trail of the evil pirates.

Suddenly there came the most enormous bang. The pirate ship below had fired its cannon. The blast scattered the children in different directions. Tinker Bell hated Wendy so much that she pretended to guide her to safety — instead she led her into terrible danger.

Below on the island, Peter's Lost Boys were looking up into the sky. They saw Wendy and thought she was a bird. "Peter wants you to shoot Wendy," cried Tinker Bell.

So the biggest boy took his bow and arrow and shot Wendy through the heart. She fluttered down from the sky and landed on the ground. Luckily the arrow had struck into the acorn-shaped button Peter had given her, and she was quite unharmed.

Peter was so angry, he banished the wicked Tinker Bell for a whole week, which made her hate Wendy even more.

Eagerly the Lost Boys led Wendy to their secret home underground. To reach it, they squeezed through holes in certain tree trunks, then slid down into a huge cave below.

Wendy, John and Michael lived with the Lost Boys for weeks. Wendy did their washing, cooked all their meals, and told them stories like a real mother.

She told such lovely stories about her home and her mother that John and Michael wanted to go back home.

The Lost Boys begged to be allowed to go there too. This hurt Peter's feelings. He was afraid to leave Never-Never Land for good, in case he grew up. However, he told Tinker Bell to guide them back home over the sea. Then sadly he shook hands with Wendy.

"Promise you will drink your glass of medicine every night when I am gone." The words were hardly out of her mouth, when the air was filled with a bloodcurdling scream.

The pirates were attacking the Indians in the forest above the Lost Boys' home. It was a bitter battle, and sad to say, the pirates won. The Lost Boys, however, thought their friends the Indians had won. So one by one they climbed out of their secret cave.

The evil pirates were waiting; they pounced on them and captured them all. They tied everyone up and took them aboard the Jolly Roger. But Captain Hook stayed behind. He was out to kill Peter Pan! He peered down all the hollow trees until he spied Peter asleep in the secret cave below. He squeezed his arm down the tree trunk and slipped five drops of deadly poison into Peter's medicine glass that Wendy had left.

Later that night, Peter was woken up by Tinker Bell, who told him of Wendy's capture. Quickly, Peter jumped out of bed to take his medicine as he had promised. Tinker Bell knew it was deadly poison — as she had heard Captain Hook talking about it in the forest.

Bravely she flew up to the glass and drank the medicine herself. As she fell to the floor, her tiny fairy light was almost gone. She was going to die. Peter stood up and shouted in his loudest voice, "If you believe in fairies, clap your hands." It seemed as if all the air was full of noise — made by all the children in the world. Tinker Bell was saved!

The evil Captain Hook had tied Wendy to the mast and was about to make the Lost Boys walk the plank. All at once he stopped. He fell on the deck in fear. 'Tick, tick, tick'. He thought it was the crocodile.

In fact it was Peter Pan imitating it. While Hook was hiding in fear, Peter slipped on board and freed everybody.

Then began the terrible fight with Hook. They clashed swords up and down the deck of the ship, until at last, Hook overbalanced and fell into the sea — where his friend the crocodile was waiting.

What joy it was for Wendy, John and Michael to return home. How happy the Darlings were to see their children home safely.

It is said that the Darlings adopted all the Lost Boys, and that Wendy goes back to Never-Never Land every year to see Peter Pan — perhaps you may go there one day too!

THE FROG PRINCE

Once upon a time there lived a King who had several beautiful daughters but the youngest was even more beautiful than the rest.

Near the castle of the King was a large and gloomy forest. Just a short walk into the trees was a small clearing. At the far side stood an old lime tree, and beneath its branches splashed a fountain in the middle of a dark deep pool.

Whenever it was very hot, the King's youngest daughter would run off into this wood and sit by the pool, throwing her golden ball into the air. This was her favourite pastime.

One afternoon when the Princess threw the ball high up in the air — she didn't catch it! It slipped through her fingers onto the grass. Then it rolled past her into the fountain, and disappeared beneath the water.

The princess peered into the pool, but her precious golden ball was gone. Quickly, she plunged her arms into the pool as far as she could reach, but she could feel nothing except weeds and water lilies. Some people said the pool was so deep it had no bottom. So when the Princess realised her golden ball was gone forever, she began to cry. "Come back to me this minute, golden ball," sobbed the Princess, staring hard into the water.

Now as a rule, Princesses are used to getting their own way. So after her golden ball didn't magically pop up out of the water, she started to howl even louder. Dear, oh dear! First she stamped her feet and then she threw herself down on the grass in temper.

The Princess was making so much noise, that she didn't notice a big green frog stick his head out of the water and jump onto the grass beside her. "Don't cry beautiful Princess," the frog croaked. "I saw your golden ball fall into the water, and it will be my pleasure to dive down and get it for you — if you will give me something in return."

At this the Princess cheered up. "I will gladly give you my jewels and pearls, even my golden crown, if you will bring back my golden ball." It's true to say that promises should never be made in a hurry, even by Princesses, because a promise is a thing that must be kept — especially to frogs!

The frog hopped nearer to the Princess. "Pearls and jewels and golden crowns are no use to me," he went on, "but if you'll love me and be my friend, if you'll let me eat from your golden plate, drink from your golden cup, and sleep on your golden bed, I will dive down and fetch your ball."

So eager was the Princess to see her golden ball once more, that she didn't listen too carefully to what the frog had to say. "I promise you all you ask, if only you will bring back my ball."

Quick as a flash, the frog jumped into the pool then bobbed up again with the ball in his mouth. Straight away the King's daughter snatched her ball and ran back to the castle.

"Take me with you," cried the frog. "I cannot run as fast as you and shall be left behind."

But the Princess didn't care about her promise and soon forgot all about the frog. Later that day, when the Princess was sitting at the table, something was heard coming up the marble stairs, "Splish, splosh." The sound came nearer and nearer and a voice cried, "Let me in, youngest daughter of the King."

The Princess jumped up to see who had called her. Now when she caught sight of the frog, she turned very pale.

"What does a frog want with you?" demanded the King, looking rather surprised.

The Princess hung her head. "When I was sitting playing by the fountain my golden ball fell into the water. This frog fetched it back for me — because I cried so much." The Princess started to cry again. "I promised to love him and let him eat from my golden plate, drink from my golden cup and sleep on my golden bed."

The King looked at the frog and thought for a while before he spoke. "Then you must keep your promise, my daughter."

The Princess knew she must obey, so she beckoned the frog to come inside. The frog hopped in after her and jumped into her chair and straight onto the table. "Now push your golden plate near me," said the frog, "so that we may eat together." As she did so, the frog leapt onto her plate and gobbled up all her dinner, which was just as well, because the Princess didn't feel much like eating.

Next, the frog drank from her little golden cup until it was quite empty. Somehow the Princess didn't feel thirsty either! After the frog had finished, he took one great leap and landed on the Princess's knee. "Go away you ugly cold frog!" she screamed. "I will never let you sleep on my lovely clean bed!"

This made the King very angry. "This frog helped you when you needed it. Now you must keep your promise to him."

"I am very tired after that wonderful meal," the frog said, "and you did promise that I could go to sleep on your golden bed."

Very unwillingly the Princess picked up the frog and carried him upstairs to her room.

When the frog hopped into the middle of her· golden bed, it was just too much for the Princess. She tugged hard at the coverlet and tipped the poor frog onto the floor.

As he fell he was changed into a handsome Prince. A spell had been cast on him by an evil witch and only the Princess had the power to break it.

The Princess was speechless. She felt very sorry indeed that she had been so unkind to the frog.

After a while, the handsome Prince and the Princess got married, and I'm sure lived happily ever after.

HANSEL AND GRETEL

Once upon a time, there lived on the edge of a dark forest a poor woodcutter, his wife and two children. The little boy was called Hansel and the little girl's name was Gretel.

When the children were small, the woodcutter had lots of work and everyone had plenty to eat. But sad to say, their happiness did not last. The woodcutter's wife died, and the poor man chose another, who turned out to be cruel and selfish.

One day a great famine came to the land, leaving everyone short of food. The poor woodcutter was very worried as they had only one piece of bread left. His family would soon starve.

Hansel and Gretel's cruel stepmother made sure that she wouldn't starve. "Tomorrow morning, take the children to the thickest part of the forest, and leave them," she said. "Someone may come along and take pity on them and perhaps give them some food. For if they stay with us they will starve anyway."

She pleaded and argued so much that the woodcutter was forced to agree with her evil suggestion. Hansel and Gretel had not been able to sleep, because they were so hungry. And they heard every word their parents had said.

"Don't cry, Gretel," said the boy to his little sister, "for I have thought of a plan to find our way home again."

The moon was shining brightly as Hansel climbed out of his bedroom window and jumped down onto the path. He filled both his pockets with small white pebbles, then crept quietly back to bed.

Early next morning, the poor woodcutter led his children deeper and deeper into the forest.

Clever Hansel trailed behind, pretending to be watching the birds. Every so often he let fall a shiny white pebble from his pocket.

When it grew dark, the woodcutter built a huge fire. His children were so tired that they fell asleep in front of it. When they woke up, their father had gone.

Little Gretel was very frightened, and began to cry. "Don't worry," Hansel told his sister. "Wait until the moon comes out."

Once the moon had risen, the children could see the pebbles shining brightly on the forest path. They followed them, and by morning they were home.

Their father was overjoyed to see his dear children again, but their cruel stepmother was very angry because her plan had failed.

It wasn't long before she began to argue and plead with the woodcutter once more. "There is not enough food left to feed us all," she screamed. "Get rid of your children, or we shall all die."

This time (to make sure the woodcutter made no more mistakes), the stepmother went along to see that Hansel and Gretel were left to die in the forest.

However, she did not notice Hansel throwing down tiny crumbs of bread onto the forest path.

Once again, the woodcutter made the children a roaring fire, and once again they both fell fast asleep.

When the children woke up and found themselves alone, they began to search for the breadcrumbs. But, alas, the birds had eaten them all up. Poor Hansel and Gretel, they sat down and cried themselves to sleep by the fire.

In the morning, when it grew light, the two set off to find their way home. In fact, they were just walking — round in circles— deeper and deeper into the forest.

It was then that Hansel noticed a tiny white bird sitting on a branch. The bird began to sing, "Follow me, follow me." It flew in front of the children until it reached a little house in a clearing.

It was the most unusual house you could dream of. The walls were made of gingerbread and the roof of cake and biscuits. The windows were sugar and the doors were peppermint sticks. Hansel and Gretel were so hungry that they began to eat bits and pieces off the house.

Then the door opened and an old woman hobbled out. At first the children drew back in fear. "Come inside, my dears," she smiled, "and I will look after you."

The old woman cooked them a lovely dinner, and showed them two little beds covered with soft pillows and blankets. That night the children fell asleep thinking they were safe and sound at last.

Poor Hansel and Gretel. They had fallen right into a trap. The old woman was really a witch whose favourite food was children!

Very early next morning, the witch grabbed the sleeping Hansel and locked him in a cage.

107

Next, she shook Gretel hard. "Wake up girl and cook your brother a huge breakfast. When he is fat enough I shall eat him."

Day after day, Gretel had to cook huge meals to fatten-up her brother.

Now, the witch was very short-sighted. Every morning she would make Hansel stick his finger out of the cage —just to see how much he had grown. But the boy was crafty. Instead of his finger, he would poke a chicken bone through the bars. "You're still too thin," she would scream, and make Gretel cook even more food.

Week after week went by, until the witch could wait no longer. "I shall eat him right away!"she cackled.

Without wasting a moment, the old witch dragged Gretel into the kitchen. She made the terrified girl stoke the fire until the oven was red hot. "Is the oven ready for roasting?" called the witch with glee.

"I cannot tell," answered Gretel, pretending not to understand.

This made the witch very angry. "Stupid girl," she cried, as she pulled Gretel across the room. "This is how it's done," and the witch bent over and stuck her head in the oven.

Gretel gave her one great push, and the evil witch fell inside and was burnt to a crisp.

Swiftly, Gretel freed her brother from that awful cage, and the children danced for joy.

Before they left for home, they found a pile of gold hidden in the witch's cottage.

Then, as if by magic, a new path opened up through the forest. It led to a broad river where a great white duck was waiting to take them across.

Very soon they saw their own dear house through the trees. Their wicked stepmother had died, and their father was a sad and sorry man.

Luckily, Hansel and Gretel soon forgot about the wicked witch. They forgave their poor father and all lived happily every after.

THE THREE LITTLE PIGS

Once upon a time, there was a Mother Pig who lived on a farm with her three little piglets, in a warm and comfortable sty.

They were very happy together and got on very well with all the other animals. The farmer gave them plenty to eat. He filled up their trough twice a day with as many turnips and juicy apples as they could manage.

As you may know, pigs are very fond of their food, so it came as no surprise when the little pigs grew too large for the farmyard.

Mother Pig gazed at them with pride, "You have grown so big now, that you must go out into the world and build new houses for yourselves."

As they waved goodbye, their mother gave them some good advice. "Always remember," she said with a tear in her eye, "to beware of the Big Bad Wolf." So, off the three little pigs went, singing and whistling down the road.

Before very long, they came to a stack of straw. "It must be my lucky day," chuckled the first little pig. "I shall build my house with straw, right on this very spot!" Quickly, he gathered up the straw — and in next to no time he had built himself a little house.

The second little pig trotted on until he came to a wood. "How very fortunate I am," giggled the second little pig. "I shall build my house with sticks. This is a good place to live, and I shan't have to carry them far."

So, he set to work and soon had a fine wooden house, with windows and doors and even a wooden chimney. The second little pig felt quite safe from the Big Bad Wolf, so he settled down to eat his dinner.

Now, the third little pig was much wiser than the other two. He planned to build his house of bricks — and had brought along the tools to do the job. He worked very hard for a long time before his house was finished and he was safe inside.

All this time, the Big Bad Wolf had been keeping his eye on the three little pigs.

Sure enough, one dreadful day, the Big Bad Wolf came knocking on the first little pig's door and said, "Little pig, little pig, can I come in?"

"Not by the hair on my chinny, chin chin, you canno come in," squealed the first little pig.

"Then I'll huff and I'll puff and I'll blow your house down," said the wolf. So he huffed and he puffed, and in no time at all the straw house had blown away — and the wolf gobbled up the first little pig.

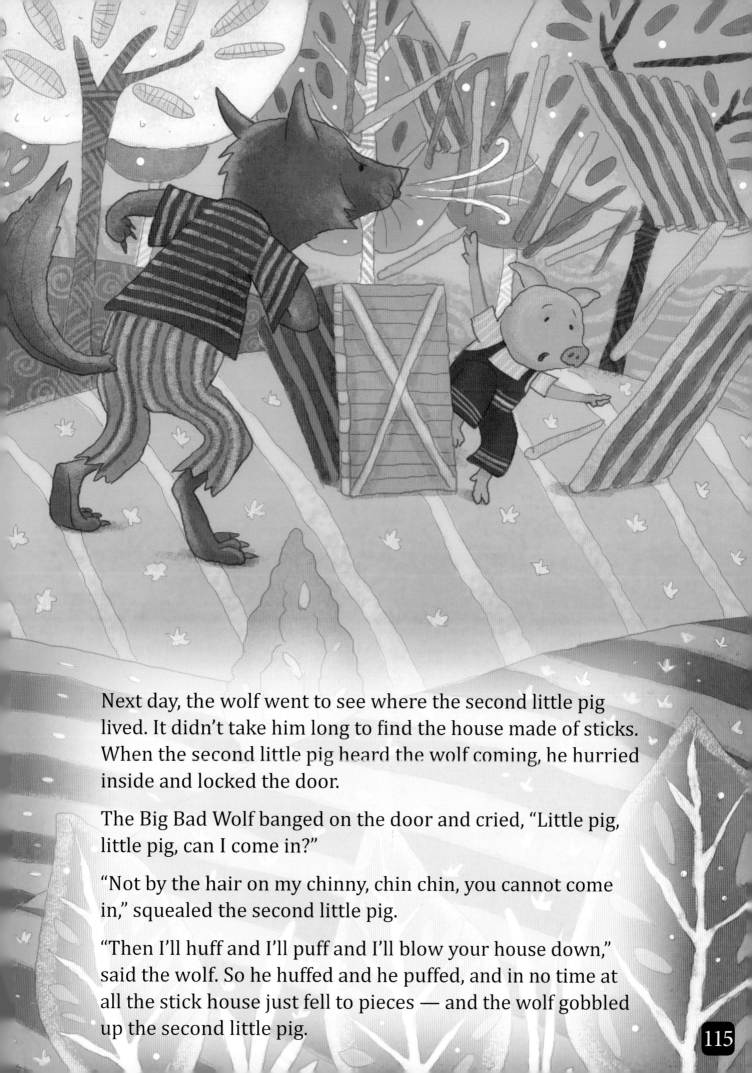

Next day, the wolf went to see where the second little pig lived. It didn't take him long to find the house made of sticks. When the second little pig heard the wolf coming, he hurried inside and locked the door.

The Big Bad Wolf banged on the door and cried, "Little pig, little pig, can I come in?"

"Not by the hair on my chinny, chin chin, you cannot come in," squealed the second little pig.

"Then I'll huff and I'll puff and I'll blow your house down," said the wolf. So he huffed and he puffed, and in no time at all the stick house just fell to pieces — and the wolf gobbled up the second little pig.

It wasn't very long before the wolf found the brick house built by the third little pig. He marched up the path and banged on the door, "Little pig, little pig, can I come in?"

"Not by the hair on my chinny, chin chin, you cannot come in," squealed the third little pig.

"Then I'll huff and I'll puff and I'll blow your house down," said the wolf. So he huffed and he puffed — but the brick house did not fall down.

The furious wolf ran at the house and banged and kicked the walls, trying to knock them down. But still the brick house did not fall in. So the wolf had to give up and go home.

"I haven't seen the last of him," the little pig thought to himself. And, of course, he was right.

That crafty wolf made his mind up to trick the last little pig and make a tasty meal of him. So the very next day the wolf shouted through the little pig's window, "Come with me tomorrow morning at six o'clock and we will dig some turnips for ourselves from the farmer's field ."

But, the clever pig got up an hour early and when the wolf called him, he was inside his brick house, eating the turnips.

Then, the wolf said, "Meet me at five tomorrow morning and we can pick apples together from that tree over there."

At four the next morning, the little pig climbed the tree to pick apples. But just as he reached the top, he saw the wolf waiting underneath — ready to eat him.

"These apples are so juicy," called the little pig, throwing one far from the tree. And while the wolf ran for the apple, the clever little pig jumped down and ran all the way home.

Still that Big Bad Wolf wouldn't give up. "Come with me to the fair at four this afternoon," he begged the little pig.

So at two o'clock the third little pig trotted off to the fair to ride on the roundabouts and swings. As he had some money left, he bought himself a butterchurn.

On his way home, as he reached the top of the hill, he spied the wolf coming towards him. So he jumped inside the butterchurn.

It toppled over and began to roll down the hill. Faster and faster it went, until it rolled right over the wolf and knocked him flat. The little pig ran home, shaken, but safe and sound.

Later that night the little pig heard a noise on his roof!
It was the Big Bad Wolf!

"I am going to climb down your chimney and eat you up,"
the wolf shouted, as he began to climb down.

Quick as he could, the little pig took the lid off a huge pot
boiling on his fire. The Big Bad Wolf came sliding down the
chimney and fell with a splash straight into the boiling pot.

And that, I'm happy to say, was the end of him.

But it wasn't the end of the third little pig. He was far
too clever for that Big Bad Wolf.

PIED PIPER OF HAMELIN

Long, long ago in Hamelin Town, Germany, something happened almost too strange to tell. Nevertheless, this story has been passed down through generations of parents to their children — until it has become a legend.

The town of Hamelin lay on the banks of the River Weser. It was a very pleasant place to live. The people of the town were prosperous and had more than enough to eat. Their pantries and larders were, piled high with rich, tasty food, and their cellars were packed with the best wines. They wore the finest clothes of velvet trimmed with fur, and shoes of the softest leather.

But one night, all this came to an end! As the people slept safe and warm in their beds, suddenly, without any warning, the whole town was overrun by rats. They swarmed over the high town walls by the thousands. They scurried down the dark streets pouring into houses through cellars and drains. Their rustling and squeaking quickly aroused the townsfolk. They jumped out of bed in horror, to find great black rats clambering up the stairs and running over their bedroom floors.

Soon, the whole town was awake, and lights began to appear in every window. It didn't take the people long to realise they had

been completely invaded by a sea of rats. They tried in vain to drive them out of their houses, chasing them out with sticks and pokers, in fact, anything they could lay their hands on. But it was no good!

To make matters worse, the plague of rats began to eat everything in sight. They gobbled all the food from the tables. They ran across the kitchen stoves and ate the stew and soup straight from the bubbling pans. There were rats in the flour sacks, rats in the milk chums, and every scrap of butter and cheese vanished in a trice. They even stole the loaves of hot bread baking in the ovens! It wasn't long before every scrap of food in the town had disappeared, eaten by the rats. The shops were all empty, even the taverns had no food or drink left.

Everyone began to feel hungry for the first time, and they were worried that they might soon starve. Something must be done! The people of Hamelin were desperate. Groups of them gathered on street corners muttering and complaining. Then they started to march through the town, joining together until they formed a great crowd outside the Town Hall, where everyone began to shout for the Mayor.

The crowd sounded so angry that the Mayor's knees knocked together with fright. He had been locked in his chamber with all the town councillors for days. Not one of them could think of a solution.

All at once the crowd grew quiet. A stranger appeared from nowhere, stepped up to the Town Hall, knocked on the Mayor's door and went inside! He was the strangest figure — his queer long coat, from heel to head, was half of yellow and half of red. He himself was tall and thin, with sharp blue eyes, each like a pin.

The stranger spoke up, "If I rid your town of rats, will you give me a thousand gilders?" The Mayor stared in astonishment, "I will give you not one thousand gilders, but fifty thousand!"

Around the stranger's neck hung a pipe. "People call me the Pied Piper," he said, and without another word he stepped into the street and started to play. He had only uttered three notes, when the rats began to appear. They poured out of the houses and into the streets in their thousands, following the music as if they were bewitched. Through the streets the Piper led the rats, out of the town gates, until he came to the banks of the River Weser.

There the Pied Piper stopped his playing, and as if with one accord, the rats jumped into the river and were drowned! A mighty cheer went up from all the townsfolk watching from the walls. How they cheered the Pied Piper as he went back to collect his reward from the Mayor.

As he reached the Town Hall the Mayor shouted from the steps, "Be off with you, Piper!" I owe you nothing for just playing one tune." Then the Mayor laughed in the Piper's face. "The rats are gone and can't come back, go blow your pipe 'til you burst!"

Once more the Piper stepped into the street. He put his pipe to his lips again and began to blow. The notes he played were so sweet that all the crowds in the street stopped, spellbound by the music.

Then, there came such a rustling and a bustling. Small feet were pattering, wooden shoes clattering, little hands clapping and little tongues chattering. Out came the children running. All the little boys and girls with rosy cheeks and flaxen curls were tripping and skipping, running merrily after that wonderful music with shouts and laughter.

The Mayor, the council and the parents stood, as if they were changed into blocks of wood, unable to move a step or cry out as the children merrily skipped by. The Piper led them through the gate of the town. On and on they danced, over fields, down lanes, until they were far into the countryside. How the townsfolk cried and called after their children, but they didn't seem to hear.

Suddenly, the Piper turned his steps towards the mountains, and the townspeople's cries turned to joy. "He can't cross that mountain top," the Mayor sighed with relief. "He must let his piping drop, and then our children will stop."

As the children reached the mountain side, a great door opened wide. The Piper went in and the children followed. And when they were all safe inside — the door in the mountain shut fast.

All except one little boy, as he was lame, he couldn't dance the whole of the way. Unable to keep up with the others, he had been left behind.

The Mayor of Hamelin searched far and wide for the Pied Piper, offering all the gold and silver in the town, if only the Piper could bring the children back. But Piper and children were gone forever.

The legend says they went to a better land where people always keep their promises — especially to Pipers!

131

SNOW WHITE

Once upon a time a lovely little Princess was born. She had hair as black as coal and skin as white as snow. "I know," smiled the Queen, as she gazed at her baby. "I shall call her Snow White!"

But soon after the little Princess was born, the Queen died, leaving the King very unhappy and lonely.

After some years had passed - and Snow White had grown up into a young lady - the King married again. His new Queen was very beautiful and also very vain.

On the wall of her room, the new Queen kept a magic mirror. Because she couldn't bear to know of anyone more beautiful than herself, the Queen would look in her mirror every day and say, "Magic Mirror on the wall, who is the fairest one of all?" And the mirror would answer, "You are the fairest one of all!"

Now one dreadful day when the Queen asked her mirror the usual question, the mirror replied. "Snow White is the fairest one of all!"

The Queen was so angry and jealous she almost smashed the mirror.

As the Queen stood glowering into the mirror, she thought of a plan. She sent for her huntsman and ordered him to kill Snow White. The huntsman wished he had not been chosen to do such a dreadful thing, but he dare not disobey the wicked Queen.

He lifted Snow White onto his horse and rode with her deeper and deeper into the forest.

At last they stopped and Snow White begged him to spare her life.

The huntsman was far too kind to kill the beautiful Princess. Instead he rode quickly away - leaving Snow White in the care of the animals who roamed the forest.

Snow White spent all the day wandering through the trees. At first she felt frightened, but one by one the animals came out from their hiding places and made friends.

The time passed very quickly and soon it began to get dark. Some of the birds and animals seemed to be leading Snow White along a special path, so she followed them.

The forest path led to the strangest little house Snow White had ever seen. And finding no-one at home, she opened the door and walked right in.

Everything inside the house was very small. The ceiling was so low, that Snow White had to bend her head to walk about. "Whoever lives here must be very tiny!" laughed Snow White, as she picked up the dainty cups and bowls.

"There seems to be seven of everything," she gasped, as she looked round the room. "Seven chairs to sit on, seven pipes to smoke and seven pairs of slippers."

Now this was the home of the seven dwarfs who worked all day in the mountains digging for gold.

Snow White felt so tired she went upstairs to the bedroom, where she found seven little beds all in a row. She laid across three of them and fell fast asleep. And that is how the dwarfs found her when they returned late that night. They agreed not to wake her, but let her sleep until morning.

The seven dwarfs had so many questions to ask Snow White. She told them about the wicked Queen and how she had tried to kill her. "Stay with us," begged the dwarfs. "The Queen will never find you here, for our house is deep in the forest."

So Snow White stayed. She cooked and cleaned and kept the tiny house tidy. And she promised the seven little men that she would never open the door to anyone when they were at work.

Meanwhile, back at the palace, the evil Queen stood in front of her magic mirror again. "Magic Mirror on the wall, who is the fairest one of all?" And the mirror answered, "Snow White is the fairest of them all!"

The Queen almost smashed the mirror in her rage. "Where is Snow White?" she screamed. And the mirror replied, "At the cottage of the seven dwarfs deep in the forest."

Quickly the wicked Queen disguised herself as an old woman. Next she filled a big basket full of apples. Then she chose the biggest, rosiest apple - and with the help of magic spells and potions - made the apple poisonous.

Feeling very pleased with herself she set off for the home of the seven dwarfs.

"How very lucky!" sniggered the Queen. For there was Snow White drawing water from the well outside the little house.

The old woman startled Snow White, and she fled inside and bolted the door. "Don't be afraid of an old woman," cried the wicked Queen. "All I ask is a drink of water from your well, and I will give you my rosiest apple in return."

Snow White foolishly opened the window and held out her hand. The wicked Queen smiled. As soon as Snow White took one bite of the poisoned apple - she fell to the ground dead!

No sooner had the Queen returned to the Palace, than she pulled off her disguise and stood in front of her magic mirror.

"You are the fairest of them all," the mirror told her. "Then Snow White is dead at last," smiled the Queen.

When the dwarfs returned from work, they guessed what had happened. Weeping with sorrow, they built a glass coffin for their beloved Snow White. They placed it in a forest clearing and watched over her day and night.

One day a Prince was riding through the forest. When he saw the dwarfs looking so sad, he got off his horse to see what was the matter.

He listened to their sad tale, and as he gazed down at Snow White he fell in love with her at once.

As he bent down to kiss her, she opened her eyes and sat up. The spell was broken. The Prince helped her out of the glass coffin and all the dwarfs ran to hug her.

The Prince asked Snow White to marry him and she gladly agreed.

The next time the wicked Queen stood in front of her Magic Mirror, it said to her, "Snow White is the fairest of them all!" That made her fall into such a jealous rage, that she fell down dead.

So the story ends happily after all, for the Prince, Snow White and the seven dwarfs - but not for the wicked Queen of course!

PINOCCHIO

This story took place when all toys were made of wood, and this tale is one of the strangest ever told. Can you believe that an ordinary log of wood could become a real live boy? Read on and you will see.

One day a carpenter picked up a log of wood from a pile in the corner of his workshop. He was just about to chop it with his axe when he heard a little voice cry, "Don't hurt me!" The voice came from the log of wood.

The carpenter was so terrified that he opened the door and was about to throw the log away, when who should come by but Geppetto the toymaker. "Just what I need," cried the old man. "I am going to carve a puppet that will behave just like a real boy."

The carpenter was pleased to get rid of the talking log, because he thought it was bewitched!

Back at his toy shop Geppetto started work straight away. First he carved the puppet's head, and an amazing thing happened ... the eyes blinked and the mouth smiled. Next he carved the body right down to the toes.

All of a sudden the puppet's foot flew up and kicked the old man on the nose. Instead of being angry, Geppetto was delighted with his talking puppet. "I shall call you Pinocchio," he smiled, "and you shall call me Father."

149

Geppetto began to teach Pinocchio how to walk. No sooner had the puppet learned, than he dashed out of the door and ran off down the street. Suddenly, a large policeman stepped out in front of Pinocchio and grabbed him.

By now a crowd had gathered and Geppetto was shouting at Pinocchio for running away. The angry crowd told the policeman to lock the old man up, for he was being cruel to the puppet. So the policeman took poor Geppetto away to prison and Pinocchio ran off home.

You will have guessed by now that Pinocchio had a mind of his own, and was going to do exactly as he liked!

Later on Geppetto was let out of prison, because he had done nothing wrong. He made Pinocchio promise that he would go to school and learn to read.

That night Geppetto made him some new clothes. "All I need now, father, is a spelling book," said Pinocchio. "Then I shall be like other boys."

At once the kind old man went out into the cold night and sold his only coat, to buy the spelling book.

Next morning, Pinocchio set off to school. But what was
that wonderful sound he could hear? It was the music of
a fairground . He forgot all about school when he spotted
a "Puppet Theatre". Without a second thought Pinocchio
sold his spelling book to buy a ticket to go inside.

But when the puppets saw Pinocchio, they shouted
for him to come up on stage to join them. The whole
performance was ruined! The puppet-master threatened
to throw Pinocchio on the fire - like a log.

However, Pinocchio cried so pitifully that the puppet-master gave him five pieces of gold to take to Geppetto.

On his way home, Pinocchio met a sly fox and a cat who pretended to be blind. They told the puppet that if he buried his gold in a certain field - a miracle would happen. A tree would grow laden with gold pieces.

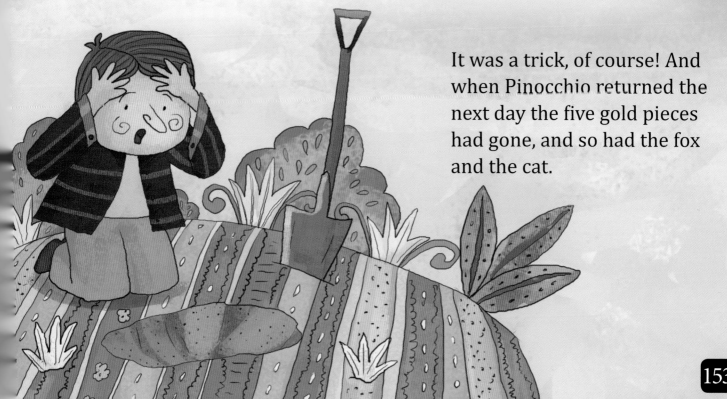

It was a trick, of course! And when Pinocchio returned the next day the five gold pieces had gone, and so had the fox and the cat.

Not content with stealing his money, the fox and cat disguised themselves as robbers. They grabbed Pinocchio and tried to hang him from a tree, then ran off leaving him to die.

Luckily for Pinocchio, the Blue Fairy lived nearby and she saved him. She sent her poodle-dog footman to fetch the doctors ... and what strange doctors they turned out to be ... a crow, an owl and a cricket.

They all decided that Pinocchio was not dead after all - he was just a wicked puppet that had run away.

The Blue Fairy asked Pinocchio to tell her about his adventures, but the puppet would not tell the truth. The more he lied, the longer his nose grew. It grew so long it stuck out of the window.

The Blue Fairy clapped her hands and several birds flew down and they pecked at Pinocchio's nose until it was the right size once more.

"That's what comes of telling lies!" laughed the Blue Fairy.

"How can I become a real boy?" Pinocchio asked the Blue Fairy.

"If you are good and go to school, you will have your dearest wish," she promised.

So Pinocchio went back to school. He worked hard, but unfortunately he soon grew tired of being good. He made friends with the naughtiest boy in the class.

One night they decided to run away to Toyland (where there is no school). They climbed into a special coach pulled by donkeys, and off they went.

It seemed fun at first, no lessons or work for months. Pinocchio and his friend loved it.

Then, without any warning, Pinocchio woke up to find he had grown a pair of donkeys ears. His friend had already turned into a donkey. All the children who came to Toyland had turned into donkeys too, then sold.

A circus ringmaster bought poor Pinocchio and worked him very hard. One day, when he was jumping through a hoop, he hurt his leg.

The circus didn't want a lame donkey, so Pinocchio was sold again. This time to a man who wanted to make the donkey's skin into a drum.

He dragged Pinocchio into the sea to drown him, but the puppet slipped out of the skin and swam away laughing. Suddenly a great shark rose up from the waves. Its monstrous jaws opened up wide and swallowed Pinocchio in one bite.

Down and down went the puppet - right to the bottom
of the shark's stomach. He felt very frightened, until he
heard a voice he knew.

There was old Geppetto sitting in a boat, carving toys
from the fish bone lying around.

Geppetto explained that he had gone to sea to look for
Pinocchio and had been swallowed by the shark. He had
lived on the food he had packed in his boat.

With the help of the Blue Fairy, the two sailed out of the shark's mouth and arrived safely back home.

Pinocchio sat down with Geppetto and told him all his adventures. He promised never to leave the old man again. And this time he kept his promise.

During the night, when Pinocchio was asleep,
the Blue Fairy came by and granted Pinocchio
his wish. When he woke the next morning, he
had become a real boy at last!

THE THREE BEARS

Once upon a time in a cottage deep in the woods, lived three bears. There was Father Bear, Mother Bear and a tiny little Baby Bear.

The Bear family lived very happily inside the cottage. Each bear had its own bed, its own chair and its own bowl.

Every morning Mother Bear got up early. She made
a big saucepan full of porridge on the kitchen stove.
When it was cooked, she poured the porridge into
three bowls and put them on the kitchen table.

There was a great big bowl for Father Bear, a middle-sized bowl for Mother Bear and a tiny bowl for Baby Bear.

First Father Bear took a big mouthful. "My porridge is too hot," he yelled in a great loud voice.

Then Mother Bear tasted a spoonful. "Oh dear!" she gasped. "This porridge is very hot indeed."

Then last of all Baby Bear sat down in front of his tiny bowl. "My porridge is too hot as well," cried Baby Bear in his squeaky voice. And he began to cry.

It was such a lovely morning, they all decided to go for a walk in the woods until their porridge cooled.

No sooner had they left the cottage than a little girl came skipping along the path.

Her name was Goldilocks, because she had lots of golden curls. All of a sudden, through a clearing in the trees, she spied the bears' cottage.

166

"I wonder who lives in here?" she cried. "I think I'll take a look inside." She peeped in the door and saw three bowls of porridge on the table, just ready to eat.

Goldilocks was so hungry she decided to try some. The first was too hot, the second too sweet, but the third little bowl was just right. Goldilocks gobbled the lot.

"That porridge was lovely," said Goldilocks, "I think I'll take a look around. " So she tiptoed into the next room.

First she found Father Bear's great big chair- but it was too high for her to reach.

Next she found Mother Bear's middle-sized chair - but it was too soft to sit in.

Then she spotted Baby Bear's tiny chair. So she sat down. Suddenly, there was a loud CRACK, and the chair broke. Poor Goldilocks fell with a thump onto the floor.

Now Goldilocks was feeling rather sleepy, so she crept upstairs to have a little rest. First she saw Father Bear's great big bed. Goldilocks climbed up, but it was so hard and uncomfortable she soon jumped off.

Next she tried Mother Bear's middle-sized bed, but it was so soft Goldilocks sank right down into the covers. Quickly she scrambled out again.

At last she found Baby Bear's little tiny bed. It looked so comfortable, she pulled back the covers and jumped in. Very soon she was fast asleep.

But who's this walking along the path up to the cottage door? It's the three bears back from their morning walk ... feeling very hungry!

When Father Bear saw his great big bowl, he began to shout, "Somebody has been eating my porridge!"

When Mother Bear saw her middle-sized bowl, she said in a cross voice, "Somebody has been eating my porridge!"

When Baby Bear saw his empty bowl he cried, "Somebody has been eating my porridge and has eaten it all up!"

Then Father Bear said, "Somebody has been sitting in my chair."

And Mother Bear said, "Somebody has been sitting in my chair as well."

Poor Baby Bear cried, "Somebody has been sitting in my chair and has broken it in bits."

The three bears rushed upstairs to see
what they could find.

"Somebody has been sleeping in my bed," Father Bear growled.

"And somebody has been sleeping in my bed, too," Mother Bear cried.

"Somebody has been sleeping in my bed," shouted
Baby Bear, "and here she is!"

All this shouting woke poor Goldilocks up. What a
shock she got when she saw the three bears peering
down at her.

Goldilocks jumped out of bed, ran down the stairs and out of the cottage as fast as she could. She ran down the path and all the way home. And to this day, Goldilocks has never gone walking in the woods alone.

BEAUTY AND THE BEAST

Once upon a time there lived a very rich merchant. He owned a splendid house and beautiful gardens. He had three ships which sailed to many countries and brought back lots of treasure.

The merchant had four sons and three daughters. The youngest was so lovely that everyone called her Beauty. The two elder daughters were lazy and bad-tempered, but Beauty was both kind and gentle.

One dreadful day a messenger arrived with very bad news. One of the merchant's ships had sunk, another had been attacked by pirates and the third was lost at sea.

The merchant was ruined, overnight he became a poor man. His two elder daughters stamped and screamed because they could have no more jewels or fine clothes.

However, the youngest daughter, Beauty, comforted her father. "I love you more than money or clothes," she said kindly. "Be happy! We still have each other."

Because they were now so poor, they had to move out of their splendid house and live in a tiny cottage. The sisters hated their plain clothes and humble home.

On the other hand, Beauty was never more happy. She cooked and cleaned from morning 'til night and took care of the whole family.

One day another messenger came to see the merchant. This time he brought good news. The ship everyone thought was lost, had returned full of treasure.

179

The merchant set out at once to bring back his fortune. But before he left he asked each of his daughters what special gift they would like him to bring back.

"As many jewels as you can find," snapped one.

"As many clothes as you can carry," sneered the other.

Beauty just smiled. "In my garden there are no flowers, only vegetables, so I would like a single red rose!"

When he came to the end of his long journey, the merchant was in for a great shock. Thieves had boarded his ship during the night and stolen all his treasure. Feeling very tired and down-hearted, the poor merchant set off for home.

For many hours along the road, his head hung down in despair. Something made him look up - there in the distance he could see a magnificent house. The merchant felt he had to take a closer look. And there growing in the middle of the garden was a beautiful red rose. "I must take it home for Beauty," said the merchant and he reached out and picked the flower.

At once the garden was filled with a terrifying sound, like the roar of an angry lion. The merchant fell on his knees in fear.

There in front of him stood a terrible beast. He had the face of a lion and the body of a man, his teeth were sharp and his claws long.

"It is death to steal my roses!" snarled the Beast. How the merchant begged the Beast to spare his life. Quickly he told the Beast all about his misfortunes, and his promise to bring Beauty back a single red rose.

"Merchant," growled the Beast. ' 'I will spare your life on one condition. Bring one of your daughters back here to live with me - or you will die!"

The merchant was too afraid to say no so he gave his word and turned away sadly.

When he reached home, his family were overjoyed to see him, until he told them of his promise to the Beast. Then their joy soon turned to sorrow.

"You can go!" the two sisters shrieked, pointing at Beauty. "You asked for the stupid red rose - not us!" Straight away kind Beauty said: "I will go back with you father, I'm sure the Beast means no harm."

Feeling very unhappy, Beauty and her father said farewell and set off on their journey. Strange to say, the nearer they came to the Beast's home - the more beautiful the scenery became.

At last they arrived and passed through the gates into the garden. Beauty had never seen anything so lovely. Flowers bloomed and butterflies danced and peacocks strutted on the lawns. In front of the fountains a table was set full of food , in case they felt hungry after their journey.

As soon as they had eaten, without any warning, the Beast appeared! He came towards Beauty, his great shaggy head bowed low. Beauty was really afraid, but she tried not to show it.

Soon it was time for her father to return home, and Beauty was left alone with the Beast.

Inside the great house, Beauty was given her own room with everything she could ever want to make her happy. The Beast had done his best to make her feel welcome.

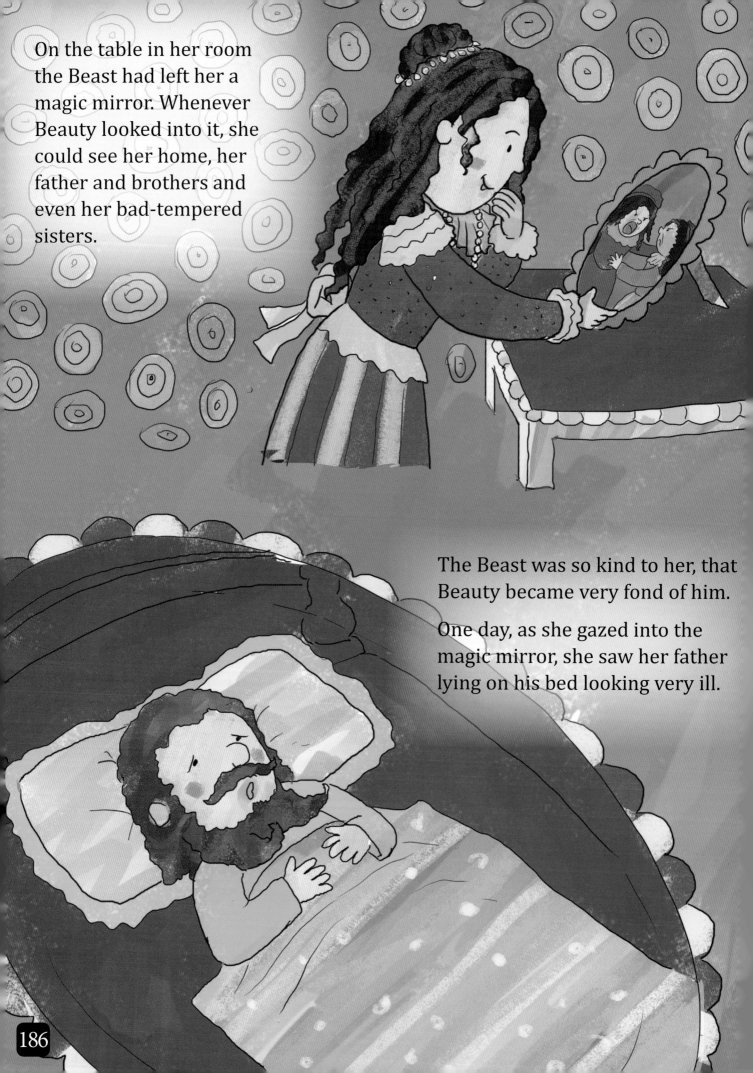

On the table in her room the Beast had left her a magic mirror. Whenever Beauty looked into it, she could see her home, her father and brothers and even her bad-tempered sisters.

The Beast was so kind to her, that Beauty became very fond of him.

One day, as she gazed into the magic mirror, she saw her father lying on his bed looking very ill.

She found the Beast at once and begged him to let her return home. He loved her so much that he agreed. "Return in three months or I might die," he told her. Then he gave Beauty a ring. "Put it on when you wish to return to me."

So Beauty set off for home, feeling sad to leave the Beast as well as longing to see her father.

Although the merchant was very ill, he felt much better when he saw his daughter safe and well.

187

So happy was Beauty at home with her family, that three months soon slipped by.

One morning, Beauty happened to glance into her magic mirror, and there was the Beast looking very ill indeed. "I must return at once," cried Beauty, "or my poor Beast will die!" Quickly she found the ring the Beast had given her.

The moment she slipped it on her finger she found herself back in the Beast's home.

Beauty ran from room to room searching for the Beast, but the house was empty. She searched everywhere in the gardens and called his name, but there was no answer.

Last of all she went to the place she loved the best - the rose garden. There lay the Beast stretched out on the grass.

"I should have come back sooner," Beauty sobbed. "I'm afraid my poor Beast is dead."

She knelt beside him and hugged him. "Don't die, dear Beast!" she begged. "You have been so kind to me that I have grown to love you."

As she spoke these words, lightning lit up the sky and the Beast became a handsome Prince.

"You have broken the spell cast on me by a wicked witch," cried the Prince. "At last I am free to ask you to marry me."

In a little while Beauty did marry the Prince and they were very happy together.

The Prince asked Beauty's father and brothers to come and live with them, but not the bad tempered sisters!

Sometimes Beauty and the Prince got out the magic mirror to look at them both in their cottage, still arguing and fighting with each other. And I expect they always will!

RED RIDING HOOD

Once upon a time there was a little girl who lived with her parents in a cottage on the edge of a forest. Her father was a woodcutter. He worked all day long in the forest, chopping down trees with his huge axe.

Right in the middle of the forest was another cottage. It belonged to the little girl's Grandmother.

The kind old lady loved her granddaughter very much, so one day she decided to make her a present. It was a red cloak with a red hood to match. The cloak looked so nice that the little girl wore it all the time. And that is why everybody called her Red Riding Hood.

But one day the Grandmother felt ill, so Red Riding Hood's mother baked her a cake and made her some fresh butter - just to make her feel better.

"Red Riding Hood," called her mother. "Take this cake and butter to Grandmother's cottage, a visit from you will cheer her up!"

So Red Riding Hood picked up the basket, waved goodbye to her mother and went off down the path.

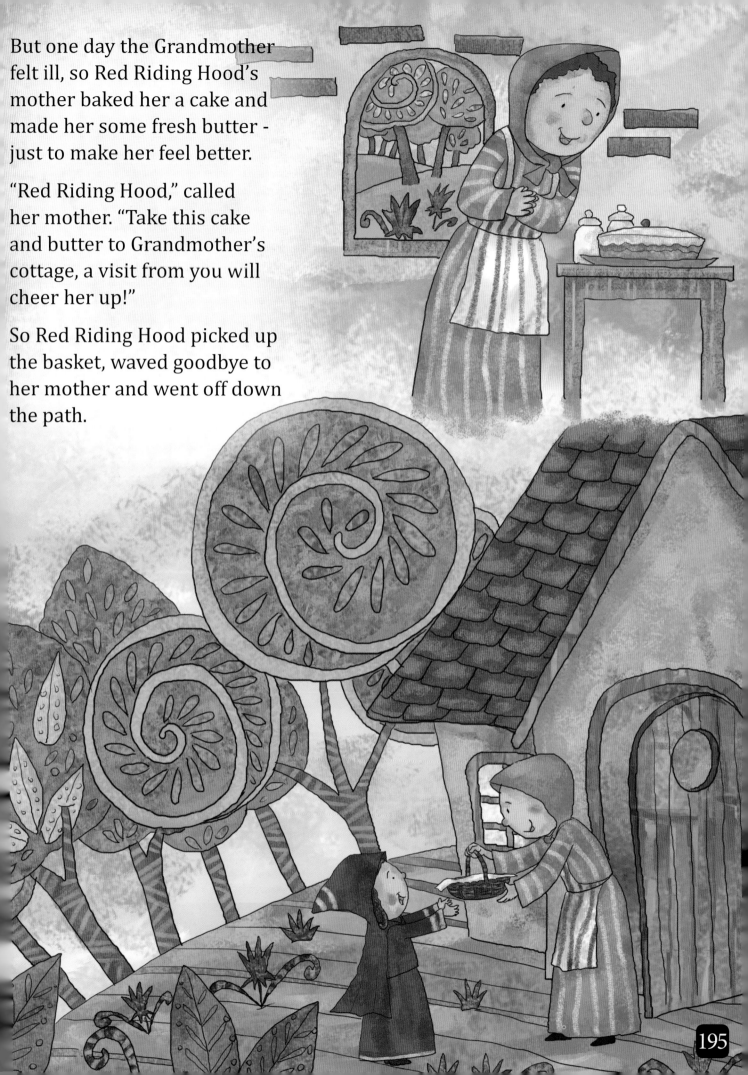

She hadn't gone very far when she met a wolf. He trotted up pretending to be friendly. "Good morning, Red Riding Hood. What have you got in your basket today?"

"I have some fresh butter and cake," replied the little girl. "They are for my Grandmother, who lives in the middle of the forest. She is ill and needs cheering up."

The wolf licked his lips. "How I would love to gobble this tasty little girl up. But if I am clever, I can eat her Grandmother as well," he sniggered. "Red Riding Hood," said the wolf slyly. "We will both go to visit your Grandmother and cheer her up. I'll race you there!"

Then the clever wolf said to Red Riding Hood, "You follow this path and I will find another one. Then we'll see who reaches Grandmother's cottage first."

No sooner was Red Riding Hood out of sight than the wolf ran off at top speed.

As for Red Riding Hood, she wandered slowly along the path picking flowers and wild strawberries for her Grandmother. She had forgotten all about the race.

That wicked wolf knew every secret path and short cut in the forest. He ran so fast, the animals and birds never even noticed him.

Quietly he crept round a clearing in the trees where the woodcutter was chopping wood. On and on he raced until he came to the middle of the forest.

The wolf reached Grandmother's cottage in next to no time. He ran up the path and knocked on the door.

"Who is that?" cried Grandmother from her bed. "It is Red Riding Hood," replied the wolf in his softest voice.

"Lift the latch and come right in," the old lady called, "the door isn't locked, my dear." The wolf bounded in and swallowed poor Grandmother in one bite!

"That was delicious," sighed the wicked wolf, smacking his lips. "Now for Red Riding Hood!"

The wolf looked round the bedroom. He found one of Grandmother's spare nightdresses and her nightcap, so he put them on as fast as he could.

Then he noticed a spare pair of Grandmother's glasses, so he stuck them on the end of his nose. Then the wolf jumped into bed and waited for Red Riding Hood.

At last the little girl reached the cottage door and tapped very gently. "Who is it?" asked the wolf (trying to sound like Grandmother).

"It's Red Riding Hood and I've brought you some cake and fresh butter."

The wolf grinned. "Lift the latch and walk right in," he croaked. So Red Riding Hood opened the door and came inside. "You sound very strange," called Red Riding Hood up the stairs to her Grandmother. "I have a cold, my dear!" the wolf replied. "Come upstairs so that I can see you."

Little Red Riding Hood was rather shocked when she saw her Grandmother. She looked so different.

"Why, Grandmother, what strong arms you have!" said the little girl.

"All the better to hug you with!" replied the wolf.

"Why, Grandmother, what big ears you have!" said Red Riding Hood.

"All the better to hear you with!" the wolf cried. "Why, Grandmother, what big eyes you have!" said Red Riding Hood staring at him.

"All the better to see you with!" the wolf grinned.

"Why, Grandmother, what big teeth you have!" gasped Red Riding Hood.

"All the better to EAT you with!" snarled the wolf. And he threw back the bed clothes and leapt out of bed.

Poor Red Riding Hood screamed at the top of her voice, as the wolf tried to grab her and gobble her up. She escaped from the bedroom and dashed down the stairs - the hungry wolf close behind!

Now, Red Riding Hood's father was chopping wood nearby and he heard the little girl's screams.

The woodcutter grabbed his huge axe and ran towards the cottage. He saw the wolf chasing Red Riding Hood and guessed what had happened. The brave woodcutter raised his axe and chopped the wolf in two with one blow. The wolf fell dead, and Red Riding Hood was saved.

The frightened little girl
ran to her father and
kissed and hugged him.

But what a surprise they got when they turned round ...
there stood Grandmother safe and sound! Because
the woodcutter had chopped the wolf in two,
Grandmother was able to climb out quite unharmed.

205

So all three went back inside the cottage. They unpacked the basket Red Riding Hood had brought and had some cake spread with fresh butter.

Little Red Riding Hood never again went walking in the forest alone. And Grandmother took great care to lock her cottage door.

CINDERELLA

Once upon a time, there lived a Baron whose wife died, leaving him to bring up their little girl.

A few years later, when his daughter had grown into a beautiful young lady, the Baron married again. But sadly, soon after, he became ill and died.

His second wife was mean and cruel with a very nasty temper. And to make matters worse, she had two daughters of her own who were even worse than she was. One was very fat, one was very thin and both of them were extremely ugly. In fact, people called them the Ugly Sisters - behind their backs of course!

After the Baron's death, his daughter was treated like a servant by the stepmother and her two ugly girls. They forced her to do all the rough work in the house. The poor girl toiled from dawn to dusk, scrubbing floors and washing greasy pots and pans.

The hardest job of all was cleaning out the many fire-grates in the castle. The cinders and soot marked the girl's dress, her hands got grubby and there were black smudges on her nose. That is why the Ugly Sisters unkindly nicknamed her Cinderella. At night, when all her work was done, Cinderella would sit by the kitchen fire warming her toes near the cinders before she went upstairs to her cold attic room.

One day at the Royal Palace the King's son announced that he was to give a splendid ball. To their great joy Cinderella's two stepsisters received an invitation. "You must make us both new ball gowns at once!" one sister yelled at Cinderella. "And do our hair to make us look more beautiful," screeched the other.

This meant that Cinderella had even more work to do. All day long she stitched and sewed. Every pleat, every frill and every bit of lace had to be just right. Not to mention the extra washing, starching and ironing of all their frilly petticoats.

In spite of all the lovely clothes Cinderella had made them, the two sisters still looked dreadfully ugly. At last the coach arrived to take the Ugly Sisters to the ball. Not one word of thanks did Cinderella get! The nasty pair pushed and shoved their way into their seats, and drove off with their noses in the air.

Sadly, Cinderella went back into the kitchen to sit by the fire. All of a sudden, a log on the fire burst into flames filling the kitchen with light. In the brightness Cinderella noticed, for the first time, a little old lady in a cloak and pointed hat - standing right next to her.

"I am your Fairy Godmother," she said kindly, "and you are going to the ball!"

Cinderella was too surprised to speak. She had no idea she had a Fairy Godmother.

"Now quickly," the fairy said, "go into the garden and fetch me a pumpkin." Next, she told Cinderella to bring her the six mice and three rats that were caught in the trap near the kitchen cupboard. And last of all, she asked for six lizards from behind the garden shed.

With one wave of her wand the pumpkin was transformed into a glittering golden coach. The six mice turned into fine grey horses. The three rats became handsome coachmen, and lo and behold, the six lizards were smart footmen.

"Well, Cinderella, now you are ready to go to the ball," said her Godmother. "Oh dear, I almost forgot your dress!"

Once more she waved her wand and Cinderella's ragged clothes were changed into a magnificent silver dress which sparkled with precious stones, and there on Cinderella's feet were a pair of glistening glass slippers, which fitted perfectly.

As she was about to drive off in her golden coach, her Godmother called after her, "You must leave the ball before the clock strikes midnight - for my magic only lasts until then." And with a last wave of her wand she vanished.

Cinderella's coach was the last to arrive at the Palace. All the guests in the ballroom turned to look at Cinderella as the Prince stepped forward to greet her.

She danced so well and looked so beautiful that the Prince fell in love with her straight away.

Everyone that night was whispering about the lovely stranger who had captured the heart of the Prince. And Cinderella was so happy she lost all count of time.

All of a sudden the Palace clock struck midnight. Cinderella dashed from the ballroom as fast as she could. Halfway down the grand staircase she lost one of her glass slippers.

As she ran through the Palace gardens her wonderful ball gown turned back into rags. No golden coach was waiting outside to take her home, instead, lying there on the ground was a pumpkin, and running away were all the mice, the rats and the six lizards.

Cinderella ran back home through the night, and hid in the dark comer of the kitchen. But when she felt in her apron pocket - she found one sparkling glass slipper.

Meanwhile, as the Prince rushed through his Palace searching for her, he found the other slipper on the stairs and picked it up. Desperately the Prince asked every guest at the ball, and all his servants, but no-one knew the name of the lovely girl. The very next morning the glass slipper was placed on a velvet cushion and taken to the city square. "I shall marry the girl whose foot fits this glass slipper," announced the Prince.

What excitement this caused! Every girl in the kingdom wanted to try on the slipper. Princesses, serving maids, rich girls, poor girls, all tried - but it was far too small for any of them.

When it came to the Ugly Sisters' turns, they fought and squabbled about who should try it on first. They tried their hardest to squeeze their great clumsy feet into the dainty slipper - but it was no use.

All this time Cinderella had been sitting very quietly in the corner. Luckily, the Prince's servant noticed her. He placed the glass slipper on the velvet cushion in front of her. Gently she slipped it on her tiny foot- and it fitted perfectly. Then she took the other slipper from her apron pocket and, of course, they matched.

The Prince was overjoyed to find his lost love and begged Cinderella to be his bride. The wedding was a splendid affair, with the Fairy Godmother as chief guest. The Ugly Sisters promised to mend their ways - and everyone lived happily ever after.

SLEEPING BEAUTY

A long time ago in a kingdom far away, a baby Princess was born. The King and Queen were so happy and proud of their little daughter, they invited the most important fairies in the land to come to her christening. The invitations were sent out and the fairies set off for the palace.

When the christening was over all the fairies crowded round the baby's cradle, the time had come for them to give the Princess her gifts.

The first fairy gave her beauty, the second gave her goodness, the third fairy said she would be charming, the fourth promised she would be clever, the fifth fairy gave her grace and the sixth fairy said she would always be happy.

All of a sudden, the door to the banqueting hall burst open. Standing there was the ugliest most evil-looking fairy you can imagine!

"Why was I not invited?" she screamed.

The evil fairy shook with anger as she went up to the cradle. The King and Queen trembled as she pointed at the baby Princess.

"Before she is sixteen, the Princess will prick her finger on a spindle and die" And with a terrible cackle of laughter, she vanished.

Everyone was shocked by the wicked fairy's spell, and the poor Queen began to cry.

Just at that moment the smallest fairy stepped from behind a pillar where she had been hiding.

"I have not yet given the Princess my gift," she said in a kind voice. "The Princess will not die - but fall asleep for one hundred years. Then a young Prince will come and wake her with a kiss, and the evil spell will be broken."

That very day the King sent out messengers all over the land.

All the spindles and the spinning wheels were smashed or burned. He made a very strict law that no-one should ever use a spindle again. This way the King hoped to save his dear Princess from the fairy's evil spell.

Sixteen years passed. The Princess grew up beautiful, good, charming and happy, in fact she grew up with all the gifts the fairies had promised.

One day she was gazing up at the palace, when she noticed an open window at the very top of the highest tower.

"I wonder if anyone lives up there?" said the Princess. "I think I'll climb right up to the top and see."

Now the palace was a wonderful place to explore, because it was so big and rambling. So the Princess climbed up the winding staircase until she found herself in front of a small door. Gently she pushed it open.

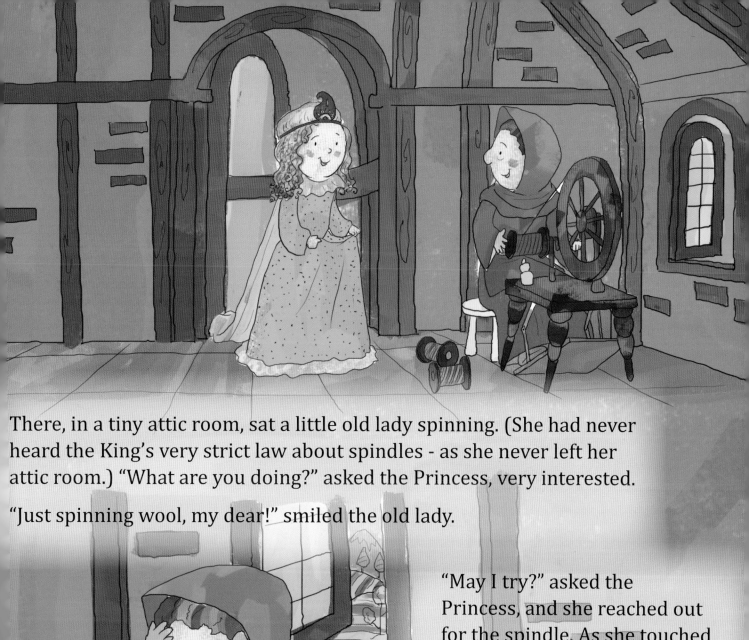

There, in a tiny attic room, sat a little old lady spinning. (She had never heard the King's very strict law about spindles - as she never left her attic room.) "What are you doing?" asked the Princess, very interested.

"Just spinning wool, my dear!" smiled the old lady.

"May I try?" asked the Princess, and she reached out for the spindle. As she touched the sharp point, it pricked her finger.

The evil fairy's spell had worked. At once the Princess fell to the floor in a deep sleep.

When the King and Queen were told what had happened, and when they saw the Princess asleep, they knew the evil spell had come true. Their beloved daughter would sleep for a hundred years.

The servants carried the Princess from the attic room and laid her on a beautiful velvet-covered bed.

Now the good fairy (who promised the Princess would not die) came at once to the Palace. Without a word she touched everybody with her wand.

She touched the cooks in the kitchen, and the servants who waited at the Palace banqueting table.

She touched the guards and the footmen, the pages and the maids.

Her magic wand even sent the Princess's little dog to sleep.

A strange silence fell over everything. Gently, her wand touched the King and Queen before she flew away from the Palace.

231

The good fairy waved her wand for the last time
and a thick forest sprang up around the Palace.
Tangled briar and thorns crept over the paths and
up the walls. This way no-one could cut through the
undergrowth or visit the sleeping Palace, until one
hundred years had gone by.

As time passed people forgot all about the Palace and the sleeping Princess.

One day a handsome Prince was out hunting nearby. He happened to look up and saw the very tops of the Palace towers peeping above the trees.

From out of nowhere the good fairy appeared! She told him of the Princess and the evil spell that only a handsome Prince like him could break.

At once the Prince drew his sword and began to cut a path through the thick brambles.

Very soon he reached the Palace. He passed snoring
guards and sleeping ladies and gentlemen.

The Palace cat was snoozing peacefully on a cushion.

There were even a couple of mice fast asleep
under the table in the banqueting hall.

They had all been asleep for one
hundred years.

Suddenly, the Prince looked up and saw the beautiful Princess asleep in her velvet-covered bed. He knelt beside her and kissed her hand. At last the evil spell was broken...

...And everyone woke up, just as the good fairy had planned!

The Prince and Princess fell in love and after a while they were married, and of course lived happily ever after.

THE GINGERBREAD MAN

Once upon a time there lived an old woman, an old man and a little boy. Now one day the old woman was so busy in her kitchen she asked the little boy to help her. They were going to do some baking while the old man went into the garden to dig.

"Let's get started," said the old woman. "We have lots to do today." She told the little boy that if he worked hard, he could make something special.

The little boy found the rolling pin and baking tins. Next he got out the flour, the eggs and the butter. He weighed the sugar and beat the eggs. He even rolled out the pastry.

Very soon they had baked a big pile of cakes and pies. They made fancy little cakes with icing and sweets on top, and buns covered in chocolate and tarts filled with red jam. They looked delicious.

"We're almost done," said the old woman with a smile. "Have a look in my cookery book and find something special you would like to bake."

The little boy opened the book and found it at once. "I want to make the biggest Gingerbread Man in the world," he cried.

So the little boy found the largest baking tin that would fit into the oven. He cut out the Gingerbread Man shape then he gave him currants for eyes and buttons, and a slice of lemon peel for a mouth.

The old woman put the Gingerbread Man into the oven, and told the boy to keep an eye on him, while she went out into the garden.

It wasn't very long before he heard strange noises coming from the oven. First a tapping, then a banging and then a very loud knocking.

All at once, the oven door burst open, and out jumped the Gingerbread Man.

He dashed past the little boy and straight out the kitchen door. He ran outside, down the path, and out of the garden gate.

The old man, the old woman and the little boy began to chase after him. But the Gingerbread Man laughed and shouted, "Run! Run! As fast as you can! You can't catch me, I'm the Gingerbread Man!"

"Free at last," he shouted, as he ran over hills and away. "No-one can catch me and eat me up because I'm the Gingerbread Man."

On his way he passed some men resting under a tree. "Can't catch me," yelled the Gingerbread Man, as he sped by.

"It's too hot to run," shouted the men, "but if you come any closer, we'll eat you for our dinner." But the Gingerbread Man just stuck out his tongue.

By now the Gingerbread Man was beginning to enjoy his freedom. He spied a big black cat fast asleep in the sun. The Gingerbread Man pulled her whiskers as he ran by.

The cat sprang up and chased after the Gingerbread Man trying to catch him with her sharp claws. "Run! Run! As fast as you can! You can't catch me, I'm the Gingerbread Man!"

The cat ran after the Gingerbread Man for miles, but she never caught him.

On and on he ran until he heard a fierce dog barking in a garden. "Can't catch me," teased the Gingerbread Man.

The dog was so startled he jumped over the gate and ran after the Gingerbread Man. He snapped and snarled at him, and tried to bite him in half with his sharp teeth.

"Run! Run! As fast as you can! You can't catch me, I'm the Gingerbread Man!" The dog chased after him until he was too tired to go any farther. But he never did catch the Gingerbread Man.

Next he passed a field of cows quietly munching the grass. The Gingerbread Man climbed up on the fence and shouted at the top of his voice. "Can't catch me, I'm the Gingerbread Man."

One of the cows lifted up her head, "I don't need to run after you," she mooed. "I can reach you from here." She was so big she almost swallowed the Gingerbread Man in one bite.

The Gingerbread Man fell off the fence in fright. He picked himself up and cried, "Run! Run! As fast as you can! You can't catch me, I'm the Gingerbread Man!" The cow went on quietly munching the grass.

The Gingerbread Man just kept on running until he came to a river. He sat down on the bank quite out of breath and feeling rather pleased with himself. "It must be true," he said out loud. "No-one can catch me. An old woman, an old man and a little boy can't catch me. The men resting under the tree couldn't either, nor could the black cat or the fierce dog, not even that silly cow."

The Gingerbread Man grinned. "I really am the most wonderful Gingerbread Man in the world."

Now hiding in the grass near the river bank was a Fox. He heard every word that the Gingerbread Man said and he licked his lips.

"Good day. What a fine looking fellow you are," called the Fox, as he strolled along the river bank towards the Gingerbread Man.

"Thank you, kind sir," smiled the Gingerbread Man. "Run! Run! As fast as you can! You can't catch me, I'm the Gingerbread Man!"

"I wouldn't dream of trying," said the Fox slyly. "Tell me, Gingerbread Man. How are you going to cross the river? Can you swim?"

The Gingerbread Man looked rather dismayed. "I can jump. I can do hand-stands. I can even balance on one leg. However, you are quite right, Mr. Fox, I cannot swim."

"Now I can swim very well," sniggered the Fox. "I have a wonderful idea, Gingerbread Man. If you balance on my tail, I will take you across the river."

So the Fox and the Gingerbread Man started to cross the water. They hadn't gone very far before the Fox's tail began to get wet. "Stand on my back," said the Fox, "and you'll be alright."

So the Gingerbread man climbed onto his back. Deeper and deeper they went. Soon the Fox's back was underwater. "Climb up onto my head," called the Fox, "or you'll get wet."

So the Gingerbread Man climbed onto his head. A little farther across the river the Fox's head began to sink under the water. "Climb up on my nose," shouted the Fox, "or you will drown."

The Gingerbread Man climbed up onto the very top of the Fox's nose. The Fox opened his mouth wide and, SNAP, he gobbled him up in one bite.

So that was the end of the poor Gingerbread Man. "Run! Run! As fast as you can! You can't catch me, I'm the Gingerbread Man!" And no-one ever did catch him ... except the Fox.

BYE BABY BUNTING
and other rhymes

Bye, baby bunting,
Daddy's gone a-hunting,
Gone to get a rabbit skin,
To wrap the baby bunting in.

Insey Winsey spider,
Climbed up the water spout;
Down came the rain
And washed the spider out;
Out came the sunshine
And dried up all the rain;
Insey Winsey spider,
Climbed up the spout again.

Bulls head

"Who goes there?"
"A Grenadier."
"What do you want?"
"A pot of beer?"

254

Cuckoo, cuckoo, what do you do?
In April I open my bill;
In May I sing night and day;
In June I change my tune;
In July I prepare to fly;
In August away I must.

Terence McDiddler
The three-stringed fiddler
Can charm, if you please,
The fish from the seas.

A wise old owl sat in an oak,
The more he heard the less he spoke;
The less he spoke the more he heard.
Why aren't we all like that wise old bird?

Little Miss Muffet
Sat on her tuffet,
Eating her curds and whey;
There came a big spider,
Who sat down beside her
And frightened Miss Muffet away.

Jack and Jill.
Went up the hill,
To fetch a pail of water;

Jack fell down,
And broke his crown,
And Jill came tumbling after.

I love little pussy,
Her coat is so warm,
And if I don't hurt her,
She'll do me no harm.
So I'll not pull her tail,
Or drive her away,
But Pussy and I
Very gently will play.
She will sit by my side,
And I'll give her some food,
And she'll like me because
I am gentle and good.

Doctor Foster went to Gloucester
In a shower of rain;
He stepped in a puddle,
Right up to his middle,
And never went there again.

Girls and boys come out to play,
The moon doth shine as bright as day.
Leave your supper and leave your sleep,
And come with your playfellows into the street.
Come with a whoop and come with a call,
Come with a good will or not at all.
Up the ladder and down the wall,
A half-penny loaf will serve us all;
You find milk, and I'll find flour,
And we'll have a pudding in half an hour.

The Man in the Moon
Looked out of the moon,
Looked out of the moon and said,
"This time for all children on the earth
To think about getting to bed!"

Ring-a-ring o'roses,
A pocket full of posies,
A-tishoo! A-tishoo!
We all fall down.

Charley Parley stole the barley
Out of the baker's shop.
The baker came out,
and gave him a clout,
Which made poor Charley hop.

There was an old woman who lived in a shoe;
She had so many children she didn't know what to do.
She gave them some broth without any bread;
Then whipped them all soundly and put them to bed.

Mary, Mary, quite contrary,
How does your garden grow?
With silver bells and cockle shells,
And pretty maids all in a row.

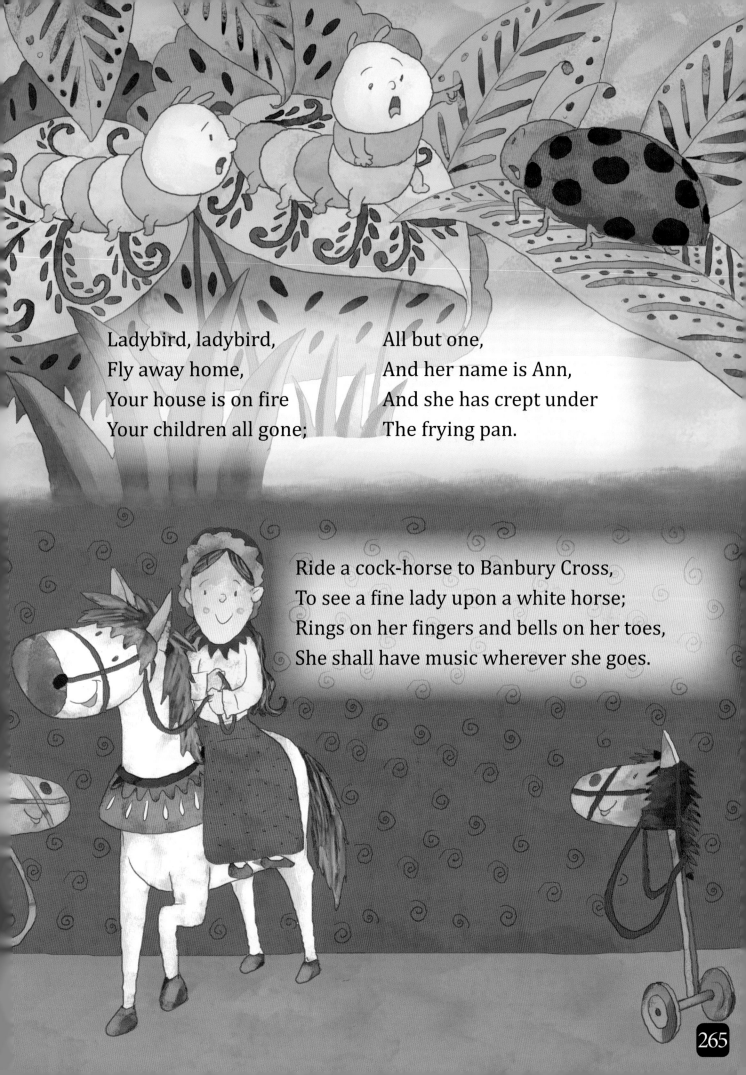

Ladybird, ladybird,
Fly away home,
Your house is on fire
Your children all gone;

All but one,
And her name is Ann,
And she has crept under
The frying pan.

Ride a cock-horse to Banbury Cross,
To see a fine lady upon a white horse;
Rings on her fingers and bells on her toes,
She shall have music wherever she goes.

Cock a doodle doo!
My dame has lost her shoe,
My master's lost his fiddling stick
And knows not what to do.
Cock a doodle doo!
What is my dame to do?
Till master finds his fiddling stick
She'll dance without her shoe.

Tom, Tom, the piper's son,
Stole a pig and away did run;
The pig was eat,
And Tom was beat,
And Tom went howling
Down the street.

Roses are red,
Violets are blue,

Sugar is sweet
And so are you.

267

Humpty Dumpty sat on a wall,
Humpty Dumpty had a great fall;
All the King's horses,
And all the King's men,
Couldn't put Humpty together again .

A diller, a dollar,
A ten o'clock scholar,
What makes you come so soon?
You used to come at ten o'clock,
But now you come at noon.

Pat-a-cake, pat-a-cake,
baker's man,

Bake me a cake as fast
as you can;

Pat it and prick it, and
mark it with B,

Put it in the oven for
Baby and me.